Jenn
Ranch!

Kicking Dust

Swallow Road Ranch

Nesi L Stone

LostStone Publishing

LostStone Publishing

LostStone Publishing

Second Edition

PRINT ISBN 978-1-0699517-9-3

EBOOK ISBN 978-1-0697483-1-7

Editing: Editing by Gee

Cover: Loststone Publishing

Formatting: Loststone Publishing via Atticus

To everyone scared of chickens.
Me too.

Also By Nesi L Stone

Series

SplinterRealm

Locked in Pleasure

Broken Magic Duet

Split Between Magic

Swallow Road Ranch

Kicking Dust

Kicking Stones (Coming Soon!)

Stand Alone Books

Broken Moon Spirit

PLAYLIST

One of Them Girls by Lee Brice (VAVO remix)
Pray by Lauren Spencer Smith
My Home by Myles Smith
Call Your Mom by Noah Kahan
Chokehold by Austin Giorgio
Ordinary by Alex Warren
Anchor by Novo Amor
Waiting for You by Myles Smith
Work Song by Hozier

Trigger Warning

Only in Specified Chapters

Animal Death

CH 26

Starting on page 249

Animals Abuse

CH 26

Starting on page 249

General Content/ Trigger Warnings for Whole Story

Explicit Sexual Acts

(breeding kink)

Explicit Language

Boss x Employee Power Dynamic

Age Gap

(12 year age gap)

Drunk Driving

This book takes place in the fictional town of Woodlow in Ontario Canada that is inspired by many small towns in Ontario!

JASPER

Pratt

Ernie's at 8.

Typing…

No….

Pratt

Don't even try saying no. I'm putting the tab in your name.

k.

Pratt

For every 5 minutes you are late I am ordering a shot on your dime.

Asshole

My best-friend, who I have known my whole life, was a dick. Dragging my ass to the local bar on a Tuesday in which we would get too drunk to drive home; yet still do it anyways. *I was not going to like myself in the morning.* But he was only in town for one week a month so I always showed up when he called. *Always.*

I had heard so many times *"Noah Pratt and Jasper Harlow had been shit disturbers since they could walk and had been terrorizing Woodlow Ontario since elementary school."* Woodlow had taken enough from me that it was only fair.

I shoved my phone back in my jeans and walked into the barn. Jackle my black shire horse stood in his pen nickering at me as I got closer.

"Ready for work?" I asked him as I unlocked his pen.

I brushed my hair back glancing at the clock. *Fuck! I'm gonna be late!* I tugged my black baseball hat on my head and snatched up my wallet and keys. I jumped into the cab of my old dodge gunning the engine before I pulled out of my cabin and down the long drive to the road. I left Swallow Road Ranch in my rear view.

I was twelve minutes late when I pulled into the parking lot at Ernie's. It was a hole in the wall shit bar but it was the best place for loud music and cheap beer. The bar was no longer owned by Ernie nor called Ernie's but to everyone it was Ernie's. The current owner was Ernie's son and it made him happy his pop's was remembered well. I ducked into the booth Noah had secured. He had three empty shot glasses lined up in front of him.

"Asshole," I greeted.

"You are late," he pointed out showing off his shot glasses.

We waved down a waitress and ordered our drinks. Noah worked with search and rescue — he work three weeks on and one week off. It was brutal work, but he loved it. He saw shit when which lead to fueling his drinking outside of work. He never talked about the worst of what he saw, but some times they would bench him for a few days after something went down —and on those days his drinking got dark.

"You work too much," Noah egged, I worked no more than he did.

"Says you," I volleyed back sipping on my beer. My eyes snagged on a woman who stood at the edge of Ernie's unofficial dance floor. She was vibrant, her head tipped back, her body loose and swaying to the music —a large pink drink in her hand.

She swayed back and forth on bright red Doc Martin's, her face lit up with the beat of the music. Noah prattled on about the drama in his family over his little sister having recently started dating a sugar daddy. Which had divided the family in half—Noah siding with the *'I think its fucking hilarious'* side.

I watched the woman float around the bar through the corner of my eye. She danced and swayed her way through two more drinks, each of which had been refilled by the men hitting on her. None of them seemed to get very far with their endeavors though.

"You need to get laid," Noah commented sipping his bourbon.

"What?" My attention snapped back to my best friend.

"You have been eye fucking her all night. When was the last time you got laid?" Noah tipped his head over to the blue hair beauty. I pretended to think about when the last time I had gotten laid was—which was over four months ago— which had been a too short night with a buckle bunny who wanted to *'ride me like a horse'.*

"Too long," I finally said.

"I bet you a shot that she's a buckle bunny," I challenged, trying not to imagine blue hair bouncing on my dick —her short shirt and fishnets pushed aside for easy access.

"I will take that bet," Noah said holding out his hand.

"Wait," A silky voice said sliding into the booth next to me.

"You need to ask two questions before you agree," the blue haired woman sat next to me smiling from under her dark eye lashes. I swallowed as I ripped my eyes from the low cut neckline of her shirt.

"First; are we talking cheapest shot or top shelf?" she asked before bringing her drink to her lips.

"Top shelf," I answered looking at Noah who looked like he was gonna piss himself laughing.

"Second; what defines a buckle bunny? Is it anyone who has slept with a cowboy, or is it someone who only seeks out cowboys?" She blinked at us not backing down.

"Chicks that seek out cowboys because their cowboys," I answer.

"I will tell you, if I also get a shot," she smiled sweetly at me.

"I don't know," Noah drawled smirking at me. I could not think; I was rock fucking hard and she was inches from me, smelling like mangoes —which were now my favorite fruit. *Fuck I do need to get laid.*

"How else you gonna know?" She shrugged smiling at him.

"Well, I was thinking one of us would end up in bed with you, and who it was would be the answer," Noah winked at her. She leaned forward the table, pressing her breasts up as she did so.

"I don't sleep with people who think a pedo-stash is a good look," she pointed to his facial hair. I snorted into my drink trying not to laugh at my best friend.

"Fine, you get a shot," I said smirking at Noah. Who mouth *'hot'* to me behind his hand.

I flagged down a waitress and ordered three shots of their best tequila for us.

"Lemon and salt," blue hair pipes up as I order. Moments later the waitress came back with three shots, a salt shaker and three wedges of lemon.

"While I have fucked a cowboy or two, it was a matter of availability and not because I have a thing for them," she said, smirking at me while she sprinkled salt on the lemon as she talked — and then she tipped her shot back and swallowed. She popped the salt covered lemon in her mouth sucking on it, completely ignoring tequila shot educate. *Fuck me.* My dick pulsed in my jeans at the sight of her hallowed out cheeks.

"Fuck," Noah groaned before tipping his own shot back skipping the lemon and salt all together. I thought about the salt and the lemon before thinking better of it as blue hair watched me.

The tequila burned my throat, which was a good distraction from the words that came out of blues mouth next.

"Good boys," She purred smirking at me. Noah choked on his laugh at her words.

"Brat," I growled at her. She tipped her head back laughing.

SPARROW

I was warm and happy, the drinks in my stomach fueling my carefree flirting. I had made my way through every boy in this bar not finding any of them entertaining before I over heard the two men's bet. *Gotcha.*

The two men looked at me in shock after I called them good boys. Strong and dirty next to me called me a brat, but stashe smirked, his eyes bouncing from his friend to me. I think he was trying to wing man for his friend —unsuccessfully.

"Thank you boys," I smiled at them before leaving the both heading over to the bar and perching on the stool where I could watch them from the corner of my eye. Stashe leaned over and smacked strong and dirty over the head.

“Another?” the bartender asked pointing to my empty glass.

“Just a regular strawberry lemonade, not spiked this time,” I smiled at him and he nodded getting started on my drink.

I watched the two omen argue back and forth for several minutes before stashe waved down a waitress, settled his tab and left his friend still nursing a full drink.

“Are you even old enough to drink?” A man asked as he sat down next to me. I opened my mouth to snap at him but he winked at me. *That was him hitting on me? That?*

“Yes, and even better, old enough to think for myself too,” I smiled at him before I hoped off the tall bar stool. I paid up my tab and made my way to the bathrooms, my bladder screaming at me from the four drinks I'd had tonight. Two of the waitresses were in the bathroom smoking near the extractor fan, giggling over one of the Harlow boys. He was *‘like fine wine’* apparently.

I slipped from the bathroom and made my way across the bar to leave.

“Hey, wait!” strong and dirty called after me as I braved the cool night air for my car.

“I never got your name,” he asked, smiling at me.

“Sparrow,” I said, holding out my hand to him.

“Jasper.” He took my hand in his, pulling it to his lips instead of shaking it.

“I was wondering if…” he started.

“I think it would be counter productive to sleep with a cowboy after that bet,” I cut him off laughing.

“How’d you know,” he looked down at his sneakers and jeans.

“Your hands,” I smirked, grabbing his rough working hands and flipping his palms up.

“Fair,” he said rubbing his hands together.

“This is me,” I said pointing to my shit box car.

“Same.” He tapped his hand onto the hood of the truck parked next to me. I laughed at the irony of the situation.

“You know, if we never make it back to a bed we *could* pretend there was no time to know about your job, we *could* bend the rules." My eyes flicked suggestively to the back seat of his truck.

Jasper leaned down, pressing his lips to mine, the stubble on his chin scraping against my skin.

I leaned into his strong body as his hands landed on the small of my back.

My alarm rang from under my pillow, I rolled over, tossing my phone from my bed. My nose landed in the curly fur of my baby —who turned around and gave my face a big lick.

"Salami!" I groan wiping my face with my hand. At the sound of his name Salami got up and stretched before jumping on me to get over me and to his bowl.

"Morning," I groaned, rolling out of bed. I fed Salami while I waited for my coffee to brew. I poured a good splash of almond flavored cream into my travel mug and filled it up with the nutty coffee. I pulled my pj's off of me, leaving them in a pile next to my bed, and tugged on my work clothes. Black denim overalls, a plain t-shirt and my perfectly worn in OG Doc Martins. My eyes snagged on my red pair of boots—the hot hookup in the back of a pick up flooding my mind.

I smiled as I kicked my door open and followed Salami down the stairs, clutching my coffee. I lived in a small apartment with Salami. It used to be an old barn, but it was renovated years ago for staff housing. I jogged down the stairs that wrapped around the building, following Salami as he sped off to his favorite patch of grass.

He ran in several circles before cocking his leg, and I sipped my coffee and looked at the early morning stars. It was early; at least forty-five minutes before sunrise. *It was perfect.* Salami barked at the crunch of tires on gravel. I whistled, calling him to me, and my happy guy came running, a goofy smile on his face.

We both headed back upstairs, Salami curling up on his bed at the foot of my bed, and I snatched up my headphones and gloves. *Time for work.*

SPARROW

The night before…

Jasper held me to his strong body. Both of his rough hands cradled the back of my head, as his tongue pressed against my mouth. The scratch of his chin feeding into the hunger of his kiss.

I smiled against his lips, letting mine part slightly —his tongue slipping into my mouth. He tasted sweet, with a hint of smoky whiskey as well. Our kiss turned into a full on make out session —panting breaths and roaming hands. Jasper's hands had tucked themselves into the waistband of my skirt. My hands were sneaking into his belt.

Jasper groaned into my mouth as my fingers brushed the bare skin under his belt buckle. I took my chance and bit down on Jasper's lower lip.

"Brat," he growled with his lip still in my mouth. Jasper pulled away slightly, his hand pulling open the back door of his truck. "On your knees," Jasper commanded in my ear.

"Yes sir," I whispered, climbing onto the back seat of his truck. I wiggled my butt at him as I settled into a good position as far into the truck as I could. *There wasn't a lot of room in here.*

"Shoes off," Jasper said, pulling my boots from my feet, he dropped them in the foot-well.

"I have been thinking about fucking you in these fishnets all night," Jasper groaned, as he settled on his knees behind my ass. Jasper gave my ass a light tap with his hand, letting his fingers get caught in my fishnets. As he closed the door behind him, the light went out, pitching us into the dark.

"Then why is it taking so long," I goaded, tipping my hips up to give him easy access.

"So mouthy," Jasper chided, his fingers pressing into the muscle of my thigh. Jasper tugged the fabric of my skirt up over my hips.

"Goddamn," Jasper whispered to himself, taking in my fishnet covered ass and the black thong under them. I stilled waiting to see what he would do next, biting my lip to keep my mouth closed.

"I bet you taste amazing," Jasper commented as he dipped down and licked the damp fabric of my panties.

"Fuck, soaked for me already," Jasper whispered as he was bent between my thighs.

My forehead rested on the window of his truck as Jasper pressed his face into my ass, his tongue teasing my pussy through my panties. Jasper's finger slipped past the fishnets and hooked around the thin strip of fabric between my ass. He tugged my panties to the side, baring the hot needy skin underneath. The cool air of his truck brushed over my now bare skin. Jasper didn't give himself much time to admire my pussy before his tongue glided over my pussy. He took a long slow lick with the flat of his tongue —tasting me. *Savoring me.*

Clearly, Jasper loved what he tasted as he proceed to fuck me with his tongue. His fingers kept my wet panties to the side, giving him uninterrupted access to me. Jasper drank up every drop of my arousal with each lick his tongue pressing into my clit. *Fuuucckkkk.*

Jasper's other hand gripped my thigh, keeping me in place and preventing me from wiggling free of his tongue. I have never felt as sexy with all my clothes on as now, with Jasper twisting up my insides with his tongue. His face was buried in my ass as my thighs started to shake, his slight growl rumbling through my pussy as he felt me shake against his face. This man was far too good with his tongue —and he knew it.

He slowed his licking as he started to suck on my clit, a finger from the hand holding my panties aside joined his tongue. With one finger deep in my pussy, fucking me, and his sucking on my clit I was so close to busting all over his face. I was sure passersby could hear my moans through the doors.

"Let go Sparrow," Jasper groaned against me. With Jasper eagerly chasing my orgasm between my thighs, ripping my fishnets and shoved my panties aside I barreled towards my orgasm. Jasper groaned into my pussy as he licked the orgasm from me as it rolled through my body.

"So mouthy," Jasper joked as he pulled back from my pussy. I groaned into the door of his truck, unable to form words in my orgasm soaked brain.

"One orgasm enough, or do you want my dick?" Jasper asked, as he let my panties slide back into place. Jasper sat down on the bench seat smirking at me. I sat down next to him, my hand running up his thigh till I reached his crotch, letting my hand rest on his dick through his jeans.

"Nah, one is good," I jest with a slight squeeze of my hand around the huge bulge in his pants. Jasper groaned, his hips bucking up into my hand.

"Brat," Jasper ground out looking at me. Folding my body up as I climbed into his lap, I ground my hips into his, letting his dick dig into my pussy.

"Sparrow," Jasper moaned, his hands digging into my hips.

"Jasper," I echoed.

"I need to be in you," Jasper begged as his hips bucked into me.

"Condom?" I asked against his lips. Jasper shoved his hand into his back pocket and pulled out a dark blue foil square.

"Good boy," I purred as my fingers fought his belt. I unbuckled his belt, pulling the zipper open. Jasper did not make any effort to get his clothes off as he pawed at my legs, trying to pull my ruin fishnets off.

I lifted my body up off of his, awkwardly avoiding the ceiling as I tugged his jeans off of his hips. His dick bobbed under the fabric of his boxer briefs. *Holy fuck.* There was a small damp spot right where the head of his cock pressed into the gray fabric. *Precum.*

Jasper got my fishnets down to my ankles, my panties coming down next. I pulled one foot through them letting them hang off of my ankle. Jasper pushed his boxers off down his thighs. He rolled the condom over his dick — the freaking monster dick he had. I lowered my body down on him, the heat of his dick sinking into my skin. I brushed my pussy over his length.

"Ride my dick, Sparrow," Jasper groaned as he bucked his hips into me, lifting slightly and letting his movement guide his dick into my pussy. My body ate up his dick, the warmth and power of him bleeding into every inch of me. It took me some time to slowly sink my full weight down on him —giving my muscles time to adjust to his size — till my hips pressed into his. I was sitting on his lap, his dick to the hilt in me, in the back of his truck. A couple hours ago I was at work, an hour ago I was dancing in a bar and now I was getting dicked-down in the back of a stranger's truck. *And it was the best sex of my life.*

While I wasn't new to hooking up, or leaving bars with people — never had it been a complete stranger to me when I did it. I took my time to find a partner and vetted them before going to bed with them. And in times of great need, I had a couple boys who I knew I could call up last minute.

"Bounce," Jasper commanded from under me. I pressed my thighs into the cushion of the seat and lifted my hips up a little, bouncing my body weight on his dick. Jasper's hand grabbed my wrists, his one massive hand holding both of mine. Lightly, he held both my hands to the ceiling of his truck as I bounced in his lap. The moans slipping from my lips mixed with Jasper's low moans.

"Fuck you are too good," Jasper bit out.

"Jasper. Fuck me like you mean it," I whispered through my panting breaths. Jasper paused, his dick to the hilt in me as he looked at me, searching my eyes for something in the pale night light.

"Ask for it and you take it," Jasper warned, thrusting deep into me sharply.

"Like. You. Mean. It," I spelled out for him. Jasper dropped my wrists both his hands landing on my hips. He gripped my hips tightly as he started to rut into me. *Fuck I am so close.* Time was lost as Jasper's steady rhythm teased orgasm after orgasm from my body.

"Fuck, Jasper," I whined, as my body started to tense as another orgasm spilled over.

"Fuck, Sparrow," Jasper moaned as his orgasm followed mine. My muscles fluttered around his dick, milking his seed from him.

We sat there in each other's arms panting the silence of the night wrapping around us. I rested my head against his forehead, my eyes closed as I took in warm spicy breaths of his scent.

"Sparrow," Jasper whispered in his deep timber. His words broke the silence spell and I scrambled from his lap. Snatching at the mess of my fishnets from the floor, I pulled my skirt down —covering myself. Jasper snatched at his boxers and jeans, struggling to pull them on, looking like he was scared he'd have to chase after me.

"Look. . .um. . . I don't normally do this with strangers," I fumbled over my words, perched on the edge of the cushion.

"I'm clean," Jasper blurted in the dark.

"I am too," I reassured him.

"That was amazing," I started, "maybe the best ever." *This was too awkward.*

"I'm not expecting cuddles in bed after this. Or marriage. I get it. I'd love to do this again, but I have to head home to bed," Jasper said smoothly, catching on to the words I was having a hard time finding.

"Perfect. Amazing. Exactly," I gushed, smiling at him. Jasper held out his phone to me and

I thumbed my number into his contacts, and copied his into mine.

"Drive safe," Jasper pulled me close for one last fast and hot kiss, before I jumped from his truck and ran to my car.

Jasper peeled off to the left —the way I needed to go home— I took to the right and took the long way home, adding an extra ten minutes to my drive home. It wasn't until I was in my room trying to untangle my ruin fishnets that I noticed that my panties were not in the bundle. *They were still in Jasper's truck…*

JASPER

Goddamn fucking damn it Jake! Between my hangover, and having spent the rest of my night awake in a hospital, waiting to hear news about my brother, my day felt like it had lasted a year and the sun wasn't even up yet.

I pulled up to Jake's office —while the jackass was laid up in bed at the hospital. I was taking on his work. He is lucky; if he had died last night, Ma would have hunted his ass down and tanned it. He had a long road to recovery ahead, but he would be back in the saddle soon enough. Swallow Road Ranch was the first child of June and Jamie Harlow, my older sister being born the third year they had run this place. While Ma and Pa still ran the heart of the ranch, me and each of my siblings each took over a piece.

My sister, Jade, took over the finances, with her husband, and as Ma kept reminding the rest of us, she was the only one to give her grand kids so far. Jett took over the care of our dairy cows and the small amount of other livestock we had —except Ma's chickens. I ran everything to do with our horses; which was a lot these days. They were the backbone of the ranch. Jake had taken over dealing with our staff, both full time and part time staff members —and lately he had branched out into event coordinating.

Which I guess, I was now dealing with. Well, Jake was still handling the events since they hadn't made it off of his computer yet. Which he could do from his bed.

Pratt

How was she?

Who?

Pratt

Blue hair…

Fuck that felt like a week ago. I've been up all night Jake's in the hospital. He's gonna be fine.

What I didn't tell him was that I was still thinking about her — *Sparrow*— and her phone number had been burning a hole in my pocket ever since she had typed it into my phone. I had it saved under *Little Bird.*

"Caleb," I hollered down the hall at the back of the man who was Jake's second hand.

"S'up," he said, turning to face me.

"Did you hear about Jake?" I asked, jogging over to him.

"Yup, Mama H called me," he said, rocking on his heels.

"I am taking over most of Jake's work on top of mine. If you could take some of the slack it would mean the world, man," I was phrasing it like a request, but it really wasn't.

"Yeah, man we got this," he slapped my shoulder with his hand. Caleb had worked for us for seven years and was now part of the Harlow family.

"Honestly, the whole week's already planned, and for the most part, it's all the same shit week to week." Caleb and I carved out our plan of attack.

I spent my morning numb as I shuffled through my own morning routine —this time it was constantly interrupted by phone calls with Ma and Pa, pivoting the ranch to run smoothly without Jake pulling his share.

All the horses were off out in the field as their stalls were being cleaned. I froze, spotting a beat up silver and gold car that was hauntingly familiar. Fuck, don't tell me she found out where I worked and came here. *Not what I need today.* You don't think she's... *No. There is no way...* We used protection. And it was way too early for her to know. *There is no way she is pregnant.*

I stalked closer to the car, looking closely at it. No its not her car —this one had a huge dent in the trunk. I let a breath out through my lips. I shook Sparrow from my mind and went back to work. I needed to talk to whoever was cleaning the barn out right now.

Gentle humming came from the far stall, paired with the shuffle of feet as they shoveled out the stall. A small frame was bent over the pitchfork. I knocked on the wooden door, waiting. They didn't stop —*are they fucking deaf?* I stepped into the stall and froze. Clad in black denim and bent over the pitchfork my gaze traveled up the body I couldn't wipe from my mind.

Ear buds blasted music in her ears, her dark blue hair falling in her face as she worked. *Fuck.* I stood there dumbfounded for well over thirty seconds before she noticed me. Sparrow turned around and let out a loud shriek as she spotted me right behind her.

"What the fuck," she cursed as she pulled her headphones out of her ears.

"Can I help you?" she asked sharply. I frowned at her and then looked down at my boots and worn jeans. My face was shielded by my hat, but did she really not recognize me? *Fuck, that might be worse.* The sound of her panting breath as she came apart on my cock in the back seat of my truck filled my memory.

"Erm, I know Caleb said he'd talk to everyone about Jake, but I wanted to check in just to make sure we are all good," I grunted at her. She pursed her lips, looking at me.

"We are good," she said, turning back to her work.

"If I didn't know better, I'd say the hangover from that last tequila shot was killing you," she muttered coyly.

"I heard that," I snapped, standing my ground.

She turned around, her mouth open to retort back at me, but I rounded the corner out of the stall and cut across to the closest door before I suggested another use for her mouth. Seeing her in my real life outside the bar was jarring, but seeing her in black overalls, leaning on a pitchfork made her look so young. *Too young. She is an employee and young.* Yet, I couldn't delete the Little Bird contact on my phone.

I called Noah; it rang through to voicemail once. *Stupid fucker.* I called again. This time he picked up.

"Voicemail means fuck off," Noah groaned. It was well past two and he was asleep.

"You know …blue hair… from the bar," I skipped over her name, it made it easier to talk about.

"Yes," Noah said, I could hear soft mumbling in the background.

"She works here. At Swallow Road." I waited for him to say something.

"I mean it's the local bar, I'm honestly surprised we didn't run into half your staff," Noah pointed out. *Not what I needed.*

"And when she's not all dolled up for the bar, she looks like she's twelve." I pulled my hat off my head and ran my fingers through my hair.

It was getting long again, I just didn't have the time to cut it. Noah laughed on the other end of the phone.

"I'm sure she is legal," he snickered.

"Fucking barely," I growled at him, pissed off. *Why did I think he would take this well? I needed better friends.*

"I'm not barely legal," Sparrow said from behind me. *Goddamn it woman.*

"What?" I asked dumbly.

"I'm twenty-two. I'm not barely legal," Sparrow repeated, one of her hips popped to the side.

Her beat up boots were planted firmly in the ground and her face had a stubborn edge to it. She stood there waiting for me to react to her statement.

I could hear Noah laughing on the other end of the phone. I hung up on him. My phone buzzed in my hand.

Pratt

22!

"Sparrow, get back to work." I tugged my hat off of my head and ran my fingers through my hair before returning it to my head. She gave me a look that *'called me out on my bullshit'*, but didn't say another word before turning to head back inside.

I settled my ass down in Jake's office, determined to figure out all the information I needed to set up the work schedule, pay roll and all the other bullshit he handled. Which was more complicated than it seemed.

It wasn't long before I was stuck reading through a very particular employee file. Sparrow had been working here for the last six months, and she had opted into the staff housing. And that it wasn't Jake who had hired her —it was Ma and Pa. Which was odd. Now that I knew she was here and who she was, I saw her everywhere.

Ma

Family Dinner!

I had been expecting that text, as Ma cooked when she was stressed, and when she cooked she cooked to feed. I sorted out everything I needed to read over at home before bed.

As I left the office and started walking towards my truck, loud sounds of laughter caught my ear. I glanced round the side of the barn, and sitting on the hood of the silver and gold car was Sparrow with a beer in her hand. She had her head tipped back, shoulders shaking with her laughter. Caleb and two of the other ranch hands were standing around the ass end of her car all laughing and talking. I forced my body into my truck, if not my mind.

The drive to the main house where Ma would be hosting dinner was a twisted one. I tried to drag my mind from what the hell the ranch hands had been talking about that was so funny; or how they got to hang out with a carefree Sparrow after work —cracking open a cold one together. I hopped from my truck, frustrated and fighting a semi.

"Jasper!" Ma came trotting out of the house holding a large plank of wood.

"This needs to be taken to the barn, can you put it in your truck?" she handed me the large plank —which was painted in bright colours with Jake's name.

"Not in the back," Ma threw over her shoulder as she headed back in the house. I pulled the plank out of the bed of my truck and opened the back seat door instead. It still smelled like mangoes. *Fuck.* I slid the plank on to the back seat banishing the images of Sparrow spread out along it.

A small piece of black fabric tucked between the seats caught my eye. I tugged it free before slamming my hand down on it, glancing around to check no one had caught me pulling a black lace pair of panties from the seat of my truck. *Sparrow's black lace underwear.* I tossed the scrap of black fabric into the front of my truck and slammed the door; later me would deal with that.

Sparrow

I woke up before my alarm. As I slid from my bed. Salami gave me a dark look staying, curled up on the covers. I filled his bowl and started my coffee. I brushed my hair and braided it before picking out my clothes; a comfortable but tight pair of jeans, with a shirt that had one of those little buttons at the top. I unbuttoning it so that my cleavage peaked through. Nothing that crossed any dressed code lines, but just enough to be distracting.

After I had gotten over the initial shock of finding out I had slept with my boss; not even gonna touch on the fact that it was the *dirtiest* sex of my life. I had gone to talk to Jasper like an adult to set up some ground rules on how we would handle it, but he had acted like a toddler about it.

Two can play that game. He wanted to ignore what happened and keep me at arms length —handling me with kid gloves when he had to interact with me. Let him struggle to ignore me.

I sipped on my coffee —a caramel crunch latte— while I spread guacamole on some sourdough; back alley avo-toast. Salami then deemed it the right time to get out of bed and eat his breakfast.

It wasn't even ten minutes later I was in my rust bucket heading over to the barn for work. As I got out no one else was here yet, and I got to work. "Cooooooffeeeee," Caleb yelled from the other side of the fence. I stood up and took the cup of coffee from him; pausing my tunes.

"You free this evening?' Caleb asked smiling at me.

"For?" I asked as I blew on the hot drink.

"There is this micro-brew place I want to try," Caleb leaned against the fence, his tall lean body looking comical in his boots and hat.

"Pick me up at eight," I said, smiling at him. Caleb was good people.

"Yes ma'am," he tipped his hat at me and walked off. I was only just starting to feel like part of the team here. I was one of three girls who worked on the ranch —not counting any of the Harlow women— and new to the ranching world. It had taken them some time to see me as more than a buckle bunny who was gonna burn herself out after a month.

The first two weeks here, there was a five-way competition as to who would get me in bed first —which they all lost, and lost poorly at that.

My muscles burned and my body ached, and all I wanted to do was curl up in bed. Caleb came strolling out of the office, all covered in dust. I turned and waved at him, smiling as he waved back. I still had an hour before he was picking me up —enough time for quality snuggles with Salami and a shower. Jasper came strolling out of the office after Caleb, and he too was covered in dirt.

Why did he have to look so good all covered in dirt and sweat? It should be a huge turn off, but on Jasper it was dripping sex appeal. The warm light made his tan skin glow as he made his way to his truck. The easy way he moved his body as he swung up into his truck spoke to the years of hard work he had put his body through.

"So.. Sparrow," Caleb inched closer nervously.

"Yes, Caleb?" I turned my attention to him.

"What's your opinion on nicknames?" Caleb asked in what was supposed to be a smooth move, but was honestly a bit awkward on him.

"They have to be interesting, and for me personally no bird ones," I said counting off my two rules on my fingers.

"No bird ones?" Caleb asked as we walked toward our cars.

"Its cheap and easy; you know with my name and all," I shrug leaning against my car. Jasper's truck had yet to move from where it was parked.

"See you in a bit," I waved at Caleb before slipping into my car.

"See you soon land shark," Caleb called, waving back at me. *Land Shark?* What was this asshole smoking? I cranked the music in my car, jamming out for the five minute drive home. Salami stretched slowly before dancing over to me, his tail swinging his back half around wildly.

Snuggles with my favorite man and a quick shower later, I was sitting in my towel, digging through my clothes looking for something to wear. I had spent too long on my make up and now was in a rush, but matching my eyebrows to the gradient of my hair felt needed tonight.

I threw on a soft cream sweater and a pair of my good non-work black jeans. I scrabbled at my door as my phone started to ring with Caleb's caller ID, with my phone pressed to my ear I locked up and jogged down the stairs. I jumped into the passenger seat of his car feeling a little wind swept.

"Ready?" Caleb asked. He was in jeans and a blue flannel that he had tucked in.

"Is it just us tonight? Or are we meeting people there?" I asked hoping to avoid sounding like I had only just realized this might have been a date.

"Meeting people," Caleb said as he pulled off of the back roads and drove towards town.

When we arrived, Caleb and I darted from his car to the bar —it had started to rain, and I had only my small purse to shield myself. We ducked into the booth with the rest of our group, Caleb pulling me in so I sat next to him. Caleb was in the middle of the sandwich on our side, and a couple were sitting on the other side.

"Hello," I greeted, waving at everyone. The evening was pleasant, filled with lots of little glasses of beer that we all tried, which half way through the evening I learned were called flights. While most of the beers tasted unremarkable, beer some of them tasted horrible. Like the lavender one. We had all laughed for several uninterrupted minutes at the taste of that one.

I skipped off to the bathroom, Clary soon joining me in the bathroom. Clary had been married to Josh for three years; who had been friends with Caleb since high school.

"Please tell me you have been picking up on the vibe between Caleb and Felix?" Clary gushed as we washed our hands.

"Right," I said, smiling at her. I pulled out a lip gloss from my bag before applying it and then offering it to her.

"We have been saying there is a vibe between them for weeks and they refuse to acknowledge it," Clary was a vibrantly smart woman.

"It's getting late. I was thinking of heading out. Want a ride home?" Caleb asked as we returned to the table.

"Actually, we are gonna stay. Would you mind giving Felix a ride home if he needs it, since he came here with us," Clary said loudly leaning across the table.

"Uh yeah sure," Caleb replied, a slight blush creeping up his face as he glanced at Felix.

"Sparrow?" Caleb turned to me, a pleading look in his eye. I paused, looking at the scared look in his eye.

"Yeah, I'd love a ride," I said as I waved down a waiter. I felt the relief in Caleb's sigh on a bone deep level.

I sat in the back seat watching Felix and Caleb sneak looks at each other the whole way to Felix's house. As we waited to make sure Felix made it inside, I climbed into the front seat.

"Caleb," I gave him a knowing look.

"Shut up," he pulled out of the drive and towards home.

“He’s hot,” I giggled at Caleb’s blush.

“Right?" Caleb drooled, laughing.

“I totally got a feeling,” I said, pushing on his shoulder lightly.

“You have to ask him out!” I almost shriek.

“No, it's not like that,” Caleb joked, but I could hear the sadness in his voice.

“Caleb, he spent half the drive back checking you out! I saw him!” I whined at him.

“He did not!” Caleb protested.

“He did! I argued. Caleb was quiet as the blush slowly deepened in his cheeks.

“You owe me a drinking buddy if this blows up in my face,” Caleb finally demands, pointing at me. I nodded while giggling and kicking my feet in the foot well.

JASPER

Sparrow and Caleb walked and talked with a closeness I envied, I missed being just one of the guys working. In my teen years, I worked as a ranch hand and moved into a staff apartment at seventeen. But when I turned twenty-four, my parents let me take more on around the ranch, and it only grew from there. But since then, I wasn't one of them . I was still family —we all were— but I was now officially a *Harlow* and no longer just Jasper.

I watched them in the mirror as they stood around talking, letting my eyes finally take in Sparrow. The way her jeans stretched over her thighs and cupped her ass, the hem of her jeans coated with mud and the worn out boots on her feet hidden under more mud. Despite the cool evening air, she was still wearing a thin cream shirt that showed off the swell of her breasts. She reminded me of the wind that ripped through these parts —wild and free, causing chaos in its wake.

I flexed my hand on the gear shift, my fingertips brushing the soft fabric of Sparrow's panties wrapped around it. I pulled out as the dust settled from their tires and eventually pulled up into my house, once again my mind transported to that night at the bar. *Would she end up in the back of his car too by the end of the night?*

I needed a distraction. *Badly.* I cooked myself my comfort meal; steak with a bed of spinach with mash-potatoes and roast asparagus. Sitting quietly at my dining room table by myself, the night around me felt even more empty than usual.

Leaving my dirty plate on the table, I sank into my couch, pulling up my play station controller and losing myself in the fictional world of my latest favorite game. I lost an hour or two farming for resources in the game before getting up to get some water.

Car lights pulled into my drive while I stood in my kitchen, and then a minute later a soft knock sounded on my door. *Who would be here at this hour?* The knock came again, and I launched forward, pulling my door open to find Sparrow leaning against the frame.

"Hey," she whispered.

"How can I help you?" I asked, trying to keep my voice level.

"Have you ever had lavender beer?" she asked, ignoring my question.

"No." I didn't know it was a thing.

"Don't. Its not good." Sparrow shook her head, her eyes wide in warning.

"Not good?" I laughed at her antics, despite the wall I was trying to build between us.

"Nope," Sparrow grimaced, she fell silent, looking at me. We stood there in my doorway, the cool night air dancing around us.

"See you tomorrow," Sparrow said, before she launched herself down my steps and skipped back to her car. *What in the hell went on in that woman's head?*

I shut my house down for the night and headed to bed. She hadn't smelt like mangoes tonight;

tonight she had smelt like sweet sage. I stared up at my ceiling, debating on when she looked better; when she was spread out in the back of my truck, or when she was stood, bent over a pitchfork, laughing in the sun. *I could not decide.*

All I accomplished over this debate was making myself hard over the woman I needed to resist. No matter how much I pushed her down into a little box in my head, she did something to capture my mind. She was a drug I was trying to quit, but she was so damn addictive.

I gripped my sheets in my fists resisting the urge to fist my cock. *Why was she so addictive?* My will power buckled as I stroked myself once, then twice. I bit into my lip, closing my eyes, where the image of Sparrow under me was painted across my eyelids. It wasn't long before I spilled my seed into my hand. I pulled a dirty shirt from my laundry hamper and cleaned myself off as my heartbeat started to return to normal.

I tossed the shirt back into the hamper, frustrated. I had been chasing the release I had found with her that night, but nothing compared. I felt like I was slowly losing control; the more I resisted her, the worse it got.

This ended now. I can't have Sparrow; she is not mine to have. Sparrow needed to be unreachable. Tomorrow, I would throw out her panties and delete her number. I drifted to sleep my heart and head at war over a certain blue and black haired beauty.

JASPER

Four months later

I still had her goddamn panties around my gearshift; and I still had her number in my phone. Though I had changed her contact name to *Little Sunflower,* which I counted as a win. Not at all because like the sun to sunflowers, I turned to her no matter what was going on.

However, I had managed to keep my hands off of her. Every time we were left alone together —which happened far too often, considering I had managed to spend six months not even knowing she worked here— we snapped and snarked at each other like sharks.

No one had called me on my shit yet; that when she was in a group I was talking to, I'd only look at her. Or how when she walked away, my eyes lingered far too long on her ass. They had picked up on how we pushed each other's buttons, though. When Sam first commented on it in an impromptu meeting, I had panicked that they had picked up on the underlying feelings I had for her.

They never did. I mean, sometimes Caleb would give me a weird look when things got particularly heated with her. Though he does spend a lot of time with her; they seem really close.

I couldn't fully get her out of my mind. Noah had dragged me to the bar twice since her; both times I left drunk, sad, and lonely, wishing for my sunflower. Even now, as I hopped out my truck, my eyes drifted to the stairs that lead to her place.

I shook her from my mind, turning to lock my truck. A small curly haired *rat* had cocked its leg against my tire and was pissing on my truck.

"Fuck off!" I snapped at it, flapping my hands. The rat just looked at me and kept pissing. *Little fucking shit.* It stopped, shaking its small body, the jangle of a collar meeting my ears. *This fucking rat belonged to someone.*

I lunged at it, trying to catch it to see who would be getting an earful. A loud snicker filled the air slowly turning to a snort and then an all out laugh. *Sparrow.*

"You good?" she asked between fits of giggles.

"This fucking rat pissed on my truck," I snapped, pointing at the offending animal. Sparrow peeled off, laughing again pointing at me and then the curly haired rat.

"It's not a rat," she snorted, laughing at me.

"It's a rat," I repeated looking at the menace who stood there, wagging its little body standing on three feet.

"It's a dog," Sparrow said, still laughing.

"Such a good boy Salami," she praised the little nightmare as she picked him up. What the fuck name is *Salami?*

"Salami?" I asked, frowning at her.

"Yup, he's the best boy," she cooed at the little dog in her arms. My pulse spiked through my dick. *I wanted her to praise me.*

"He peed on my truck!" I shriek at her.

"A little bit of water won't hurt it," she shrugged, smiling at me.

"Keep that fucking rat away from my truck!" I yelled at her, pointing to the oversized rat in her arms. Something dark flooded her face as she slapped my hand away from her face.

"Watch how you talk about my dog!" she snapped at me, a dark frown stapled to her face. Sparrow turned around and stomped up the steps, ignoring me.

"Stupid fucking woman," I seethed, bending down to have a look at the damage the little shit had done. Sparrow came stomping down the stairs a moment later, her feet still shoved in her beloved boots and the laces undone as though she had slipped them on in a rush.

In her hand was a large bowl filled with warm soapy water. She glared at me as she threw the bowl of water at the wheel of my truck. Not a word was said between us as she stormed back up the stairs a second time. I stood by my truck —waiting, hoping— that she would come storming back down and yell at me again.

She didn't, and I was gonna be late if I didn't get going. I hung my head slightly as I shuffled off to work, not seeing her for the rest of the day. Jake was getting out of hospital tonight after four months, and Ma and Pa were having a family meal for him.

"Jasper!" Caleb burst through the office door. He was out of breath and panicking.

"Sparrow and Sam are spooking old Johnny," Caleb huffed out before running back out of my office again. Old Johnny was a retired work horse with a shitty temper, but despite his flaws, he had a permanent place here to live out the rest of his days.

He rarely got out of his stall, which meant that sometimes it had to be cleaned while he was still in it. I followed Caleb down to the barn at a brisk walk, but as the voices from the barn filtered through my ears, my pace picked up. Sparrow was yelling.

"Stop making a scene," Sam snapped at her as I rounded the corner. Sparrow and Sam were standing in front of Old Johnny's stall, the door open, and he was agitated at the two humans before him. His ears were back and the whites of his eyes were screaming at me.

"Just do your fucking job!" Sam yelled, his hand holding on to Sparrows upper arm. She was fighting to get out of his hands, her feet scrambling on the ground barely keeping her up right.

“Let me go!” Sparrow shrieked at the top of her lungs.

“Stop being a child!” Sam tried to shove her towards Old Johnny’s stall.

“What the fucking hell is going on here?” I boomed down the barn. I stepped in front of the two of them, pulling Old Johnny’s stall door closed. I wheeled on the two of them, Sparrow breathing hard still in Sam’s hands, but no longer fighting him.

“Let her go,” I snapped at him. I planted my feet shoulder width apart, crossed my arms over my chest and glared at both of them.

“She is refusing to do her job,” Sam said, finally letting Sparrow go.

“She is supposed to clean all the stalls, but this is the second time in a row she's completely skipped Old J’s stall,” Sam continued, waving his hands around like a toddler.

“Is this true?” I turned to Sparrow. She looked so small, her shoulders rounded down, looking at the stall door.

"Jake and I had an agreement," she whispered quietly.

"Well, Jake's not here," I said, frowning at her. Her mouth opened and then closed before she went quiet.

"This is your warning," I said pointing to her. She nodded, not looking at me. Come on; look at me just once. *Please, little sunflower.* I wanted to see the fight in her eyes.

"And never is it ok to physically force another person to do anything. If you have an issue, come to me. This is going in your employee file," I snapped at Sam. He opened his mouth to argue, but I glared at him and he changed his mind.

Sparrow walked away, her feet dragging slightly on the floor. Never had I seen her slack in her work, even the stupid shit that was no fun, she attacked with all she had. She never complained about getting the short end of the stick. *Maybe I didn't see what was really going on.*

"Jasper?' Caleb called as I stormed off back to the office.

"Not now Caleb," I snapped. "But it's.." he started.

"Not now," I snapped, slamming the door in his face. Jake was back; I'd ask him at dinner about this so-called agreement with Sparrow.

"How was work?" Ma asked as she slaved away at the stove.

"Good," Jett called from the dining room where he was setting the table.

"Same," Jade called from where she sat on the floor playing with her kids.

"A fucking circus," I mutter under my breath.

"What happened?" Pa asked, pouring me a beer.

"Stupid spat between two of the hands," I took the glass from him, rubbing my face with my free hand.

"One of the hands I thought was pulling their share was called out for not doing their work by one of the others, and it got out of hand," I groaned before taking a deep swig of the beer.

"Who?" Jake asked from his spot on the couch.

"Sparrow and Sam," I answered, hoping that the way I said Sparrow didn't give me away.

"Sam was slacking?" Pa asked as he helped Ma pull a heavy dish out the oven.

"No, it was Sparrow," I said. Was it just me, or did her name get stuck in my mouth each time I said it?

"Nah, something else is going on," Jake said dismissively.

"Oh actually, do you have some sort of agreement with Sparrow about her work? She mentioned it," I asked Jake, not looking at him.

"Oh fuck. Was this about Old Johnny?" his face went a little slack and Ma glanced over at Pa. *What was I missing?*

"Yeah," I said slowly, looking between the three of them.

"Yeah, I have an agreement with her. Have since she first started," Jake's eyes flicked to Ma. I waited, looking between them and slowly raising my brows higher and higher.

"You didn't give that girl shit for not cleaning that stall did you?" Ma's tone was sharper than I expected.

"Yeah. It was her responsibility and she skipped it twice." The look I got from my mother made me feel like I was a little kid getting scolded for drawing on the walls.

"You apologize to her right now," Ma snapped at me.

"Why the fuck would I do that?" I snapped, tired of being left out the loop.

"Because when that girl was hired, we promised her that she wouldn't ever have to deal with any horses," Ma scolded me.

"I did no such thing," I snapped back.

"No! Your father and I did! It was a condition of her employment! That girl is terrified of horses!" Ma raised her voice, the wooden spoon in her hand swinging through the air with her words.

"Why the fuck does she work here then?" I drained the rest of the beer, but the anger dropped from my tone. She was terrified of horses and Sam had been trying to push her in a stall with one.

"That's between her and us," Ma snapped, at me clearly done with my attitude. I looked over at Jake who shrugged.

"Don't ask me. They walked her into my office one morning, informing me of the way it was to be," Jake didn't look at me. *Something was off with him.* He came back from the hospital a shell of himself.

"I'm sorry Ma," I called to her.

"It's not me you have to apologize to." She smacked her oven mitt off my shoulder.

"I'll talk to Sparrow tomorrow," I reassured her, Ma nodded and left it be.

"Why'd they hire her?" I hissed at Jake when Ma turned her back.

"I'm not sure," Jake whispered back.

"Her father worked here," Jade hissed from her place on the ground.

"What?" Jake and I both asked, turning to her.

"Her father used to work here, years ago —she would have been, what? Six when he left here? He worked here for years," Jade said as she waved a stuffed toy in front of her youngest.

"I'm not sure why he left," Jade frowned, before shrugging and returning her attention to her child.

"He died," Ma said quietly from behind us. I looked at Jake who had gone pale.

"He left because he was in the hospital; he passed away two weeks after that," Ma said as she placed dishes on the table. She looked sad, thinking back to what had to be one of the first employees at Swallow Road Ranch.

"Dinners ready!" Ma called a moment later, back to her usual self.

We were all quiet throughout dinner. I left early and had half a mind to see if Sparrow was still up.

Sparrow

Stupid fucking men! Stupid fucking Jasper! Stupid fucking Jake! I was curled up around my now damp pillow. Salami was curled up behind my knees, his warm body pressing into me. My tears had tried to my face, leaving it feeling tight and itchy. I was sure I looked like a wreck —face all puffy and red.

I had made a huge scene —so many people had seen— at work in front of my coworkers and boss. I had made a huge fool of myself in front of Jasper. My room was dark, my work clothes on the floor, my dinner half-cooked sitting on the counter.

I had come home and fallen into bed and cried. Then, I got up and tried to get on with my evening— my hands had shook so hard I couldn't do anything. Then I got angry, and that made me cry even more. *I was fucking exhausted.*

I had curled up to take a nap, but sleep never came, and slowly the anger turned into a sad numbness. The numbness had stayed with me. The numbness was familiar. The numbness of my childhood had protected me from my pain. Only later would I feel it ten fold; but from that pain I had bloomed into the bold unapologetic person I had become. But now, in my small apartment, I was wrapped back up in my numbness.

The silence was broken by a knock on my door. I let out a sigh, blinking slowly —my only reaction to the sound. I waited for them to leave, feeling only a little sad at that thought of them being gone. Then another knock sounded through the door.

"I know you are in there. I can hear your rat," Jasper's smooth voice said through the door. *He's not a rat.* I sat up, rubbing my face, and shuffled over to the door, letting it swing open only a crack.

"He is not a rat," I whispered through the gap.

"Can we talk?" Jasper stood in the hall. *Looking like a goddamn snack.* He was in clean jeans, the toes of his worn work boots peeking out from under them. His slightly too big black hoodie swallowed his broad shoulders, hiding the muscles that I still remembered the feeling of digging my nails into, and his pinch front black hat tilted down over his face. *He was feeling insecure.* Over the months working with him I had picked up on some of his tells.

"Fine," I sighed, stepping out into the hall with him. I closed the door behind me, shutting my shame away. My bright mismatched socks stood less than a foot from his boots. I looked up at him, my arms folded over my chest.

"Can I come in?" he asked, pointing to my closed door.

"No," I said tartly. His large hand came up to cup the back of his neck before tugging at the long strands of his hair.

"Sparrow," he started, not looking at me, his eyes glued on my socks instead.

"Jasper," I echoed.

"I am sorry. I did not know," he muttered, beating around the bush with his words.

"Didn't know what?" I asked dumbly, my stubborn streak breaking through the numbness in my heart. I cocked my eyebrow at him, letting one side of my mouth tip up. Finally his eyes settled on my face.

"I didn't know you had an agreement with Jake," he said, but there was a spark of amusement in his eyes.

"Ok. Apology not accepted," I said, shrugging and turning to open my door. As I opened the door, I turned and threw a smirk at him over my shoulder. The little fire of feeling that pressing Jasper's buttons had lit inside of me died as I stepped back into my apartment. Jasper groaned from behind me.

"Not accepted?" Jasper asked, stepping forward, not giving up so easily. I stopped trying to bar him from entering. Salami got up from bed and ran towards us, his body wiggling as he walked excitedly over to greet *his* guest.

"Yes, what you did hurt me. You apologized, but I don't accept. Just because you apologized doesn't mean I owe you forgiveness," I said to him, but it lacked the bite I had meant to use.

"So how do I get your forgiveness?" Jasper asked, stepping forward, his distinctly masculine frame almost touching mine. I stepped back, getting caught up in him.

Jasper took the opportunity to step into my apartment smiling at me —with an annoying amount of pride. *Cocky asshole.* His smile almost screamed; 'one point to me'. *Two can play this at game.*

"I mean, I remember a particularly good night in the back of someone's truck. . ." I tapped my finger to my lips, pretending to think. Jasper's hand darted out and slammed my door behind him.

"What are you asking Sparrow?" He purred, his voice low and gravelly. I didn't answer; just smiled at him. He looked away from me, a small noise getting caught in his throat. As his eyes wandered over my unkempt space, his eyes stopped at my half-made dinner.

"I'm not asking anything," I whispered, taking a half a step towards him and drawing his attention back to me.

He looked back at me, his eyes lazily dancing over my body, the heat in his eyes scorching.

"Do you remember?" I breathed, my stomach pitching at his gaze.

"Every night," he admitted before his hands snapped up to my waist. Between one breath and the next, he had dragged me against him. His lips brushing mine.

"I can't, Sparrow," he whispered against my lips, his hard body pressing into mine.

"Just for tonight; as an apology," I whispered, the words breathing out the restraint in him. His hands slipped down to my ass, his lips meeting mine. He tasted like liquor and salt and something that wasn't a flavour at all. Something distinctly Jasper. I melted into him, the hardness of his body, the softness of his touch.

"We shouldn't," Jasper whispered, trying to convince himself. I let my hand fall down, the tip of my finger resting on his belt. I smirked against his lips.

"Oh, really?" I asked as my finger tip gently tugged in his belt loops pulling his hips into mine. He groaned into my mouth as the pressure of my body settled against his hips, and the boner in his jeans.

"Sunflower," Jasper mumbled as he pressed a kiss to my shoulder. Jasper leaned forward slightly pressing his boner into my hips again.

"Hmm," I hummed, distracted. *Sunflower?* We both froze, tangled in each other; the clattering sound of someone stomping around in the hall sounded. *We weren't alone —not really.*

"I should go," Jasper pulled himself from me. The spell was broken and we were slowly tumbling back to reality where we ignored one another. The cold numbness came tumbling back through me, and Jasper paused before the closed door, glancing back at me, something dark and sad in his eyes.

"Make sure to eat something," he nodded at my half-cooked dinner still on the counter before disappearing into the hall.

I stood there looking at the closed door for a moment before turning to the counter. *Was the food even good still?* I just stood there looking at it. I felt nothing until anger suddenly ripped through me —pissed that it was so easy to lose the person I had worked so hard to become. I had lost my spark so easily, and now would have to fight tooth and nail to get back. It pissed me off.

I had been robbed of so much already, and yet *he* still took more —*even now.*

Fuck this. I grabbed the uncooked food off my counter, throwing each item into the garbage across the room. I kissed Salami on the head before storming from my apartment. I was done being numb. My blood boiled as I made the short drive to Jasper's cabin.

The lights were still on, his truck still ticking as it cooled down. I stormed to his door and pounded on it.

"What the hell?" Jasper growled as he ripped the door open.

"Make me," I snapped at his face.

"Make you what?" he asked, sounding pissed off.

"You want me to eat? Feed me yourself!" I held my ground defiantly, while he just stood there, looking at me shocked.

Without a word he stepped aside, letting me into his house, his eyes sweeping his front yard. He was checking to see if anyone had seen me enter his place. He then gently closed the door behind me. My body jerked as he grabbed me by my waist, and turned me in his arms, my back hitting the door behind me. His hungry mouth met mine, and his hands fumbled over my body —my hair getting caught in his fingers. He cupped my head, tilting my head back my hair that was still tangled in his fingers.

His body pressed mine to the door as his tongue darted out his mouth and slipped into mine. We were starved, only finding salvation in each other. His body lifted from mine only long enough to pull his hoodie off over his head. I drank in his bare chest, the tan skin over his muscles slightly scarred. He looked like he had been carved from the earth that he worked on.

His hands came back to me, one arm wrapped around my hips, as the other slid down to my knee. I looped my arms around his neck as he pulled me from the floor and into his arms. My legs wrapped around hips. Jasper stumbled up the stairs with me clinging to him, laughing. We tumbled into his dark room, falling onto his soft bed.

"Sparrow," he whispered into the darkness.

"Jasper," I breathed. He leaned over, turning the lamp on his side table on, bathing the room in a soft glow. Jasper tugged the zipper of my hoodie down, revealing the thin tank top underneath. Jasper groaned as he took in the soft curve of my breasts —my nipples little buds poking through the fabric.

"No bra," he whispered as his hand cupped my boobs through the fabric.

"No panties either," I whispered, smiling at him devilishly. His eyes lit up with desire as he abandoned my shirt, and his hands drifted to the waistband of my sweat pants. He peeled my pants from my legs, revealing the bare skin underneath. Jasper smirked at the secret hidden under the fabric —that I indeed was not wearing underwear.

Spread out on the top of his bed, in nothing but a tank top, I watched him as he pulled the belt from his jeans. The heavy fabric dropped to the ground before he climbed into bed with me.

Jasper was tall with large shoulders, and while his body was toned with muscle it wasn't the thick muscle, from pumping iron, it was the lean working muscle from spending his days on the ranch. Jasper was warm, in more ways than just his temperature. His lips kissed over my skin, tracing the curve of my neck and over my shoulder. The light stubble growing on his chin scraped over my skin, lighting me up.

His fingers lifted up the hem of my shirt as his kisses danced over my stomach. He pulled the thin material over my head, dumping it on the floor with the rest of our clothes. We fell into each other's bodies like old lovers, despite having only the one drunken hook up.

His touch played over my skin like an instrument and *fuck* did he make me sing. Jasper's strong fingers dug into the flesh of my thigh where it transitioned into my ass. Jasper pulled my legs open for him, kneeing in between them.

Sparrow

Jasper pressed his tongue flat against my core, his mouth hot on my pussy. He slowly licked from the narrow piece of skin between my asshole to my clit, giving my clit a gentle suck when he reached it. *Oh hell. I have died and this is the after life.*

Jasper's deep chuckle vibrated through my core as my legs kicked out slightly either side of his head. One of his large hands caught my calf, holding my leg gently in place as his thumb rubbed lightly over my skin.

"You taste *sooooo* good," Jasper purred before his tongue slipped into my pussy. He alternated between long, slow licks ending in devastating sucks to my clit, and used his tongue to fuck me. I stopped trying to watch the man between my legs, laying spread-eagled out on his bed, my head tipped back.

As Jasper brought me closer and closer to orgasm, my moans got louder and louder, and he was no longer able to keep my legs from kicking out around his head.

"So mouthy," Jasper taunted, lifting his head and looking up at me from between my thighs. His chin was wet with my arousal, his tongue darting out of his mouth and licking me off of his lips. His heated eyes dropped to my cunt below him.

"Keep going," I groaned grasping and his hair pulling him down towards my pussy.

"Good boy," I moaned, my hand still pressing into the top of his head lightly as he nibbled at my clit. I moaned his name as one of his strong fingers stroked me, while his mouth sucked on my clit.

"Jasper," I whined as my orgasm barreled towards me.

"Come for me Sparrow," Jasper growled as he fucked my pussy with his finger.

"Yes sir," I garbled as my orgasm ignited through me, the walls of my pussy clamping around his finger.

"Good brat," Jasper whispered, admiring the effect my orgasm had on my body as I lay there panting, my skin flushed as my orgasm started to slowly cool. Jasper crawled up my body placing a soft kiss to the side of my neck. The warmth of his bare skin against mine had need flooding my body once again. I rubbed my body against his hard one.

"Brat," Jasper ribbed, his light stubble brushing over my shoulder. I sat up slowly, Jasper's heated, hooded eyes following my movements. I leaned over to grab for my shirt.

"Anyway, thank you for that," I thanked as I moved to leave.

"I'm not done with you yet," Jasper growled, sending a pulse of heat to my core.

"I'm not letting you leave without at least three orgasms," Jasper promised, his eyes dropping to my greedy cunt.

"Oh, yeah?" I challenged, but my grin gave me away.

"I know you want a repeat of the truck," Jasper whispered in my ear, bringing back memories of that night.

"Condom?" I asked, echoing my words from that night. Jasper smirked and rolled across his bed, pulling open the night stand draw. His hand came back filled with square foil packets, and I burst out laughing at the sheer amount he had grabbed.

"We won't need that many," I snickered at him.

"We won't?" he asked, his voice dropping low and serious. I shook my head as another round of laughter rolled through me, and Jasper started to gently throw the condoms at me as if I was a stripper. I shock my head at him rolling my eyes.

"Fuck. I *need* in you right now," Jasper growled as he refocused on my body and ripped open a condom. He quickly rolled the rubber over his cock as I flipped over on to my knees. I shifted my weight from one hip to the other, waving my ass at him. Jasper groaned, giving the plumb round of my ass a gentle tap. Jasper guided his dick to my arousal slick pussy, dragging the tip over me before pressing into me. He sank into me quickly, fueled by my arousal, filling me up. *Fuuckkk. Did he get bigger?*

Jasper grunted slightly as his hips hit my ass, his rough hands spread over my hips and his strong fingers dug slightly into my soft flesh.

"You look so good with my dick in you," Jasper praised, looking down at where his dick entered me. Slowly, he started thrust into me, stretching and filling me up, and then pulling out. The sweet friction and pressure of his hips pressing into me sent waves of pleasure rolling through my core. I bit down on my lip, trying to keep quiet so I could hear the sound of Jasper's dick thrusting into me. The delicious sound of him thrusting into my arousal soaked pussy, followed by the clap of his hips hitting my ass. *It was so fucking hot.*

My pleasure was heightened by the music of our bodies. His strong, slow pace started to pick up and I struggled to keep my moans quiet. Jasper's hand looped around my thigh, his thumb running down my stomach till he reached my clit. He gently brushed this thumb over my clit as he continued to rut into me. A strangled moan peeled from my lips as my body became jello in his hands.

"There is my mouthy girl," Jasper groaned. I babbled as my orgasm ran wild around my body, pulling low moans from the man behind me. I could feel my pussy fluttering around his dick as he continued to fuck me through my orgasm.

"Jasper," I moaned into his mattress; I was unable to keep my body up, and I was laying face first into his bed, my hips being held up by his hands. Jasper slowed his thrusting as he let me recover from my orgasm, before he started to work me closer to another.

"Be a good girl for me, Sparrow. Give me another one," Jasper grunted as he started to rut into me faster. *Fuck, I wanted him to fill me.*

"Harder," I moaned into his bed. Jasper cursed behind me, the sound of his low moans, that fueled all of my wet dreams, joined in with mine. Jasper pulled my hips up to meet his thrusts, stretching out my pussy to delicious fullness.

"Fuck! Sparrow. I'm not gonna last," Jasper gritted out, his words punctuated with his now sloppy thrusts. I could barely understand his babbling as he kept rutting into me, my brain foggy with my impending orgasm.

"Fuck. I want to fill your pretty pussy with me," Jasper growled more to himself than me, but the words tipped me over the edge, my third orgasm ripping through my body like wildfire. The flutter of my cunt tipped Jasper over the edge with me, his groan loud as he came into the condom filling my ears. Panting, with his still semi-hard dick in me, Jasper slumped forward slightly.

"Good boy," I hummed in my post orgasm haze. Jasper pulled out of me and disposed of the used condom while I slowly crawled out of my bent—over position and into a sitting one. Jasper dropped down onto the bed next to me, his lips trailing down my shoulder.

He turned off the light and pulled me into bed with him, my mind and body succumbing to sleep.

I was warm, and the room around me was dark. I reached out, looking for Salami. *He wasn't there*. I bolted upright and Jasper's arm shot out, landing on my back and bringing me back to where I was. *At Jasper's.*

"You ok?" Jasper's rough voice asked in the dark.

"Yeah. Just forgot where I was," I mumbled curling back up in bed with him. Jasper's arm snaked around my waist, pulling me to his chest. His hand slowly drifted down my stomach, till his fingers rested a centimeter from the slight stubble of my pussy. The pad of his finger brushed slowly over my skin. Slowly, as his finger stroked over my skin his hand drifted lower.

"You'd look so good with my cum dripping out of you," Jasper hummed quietly in the dark. *Fuck, that was too hot.* His lips met my shoulder as he trailed a blazing hot path towards my collar bone.

"I haven't been with anyone else since that night," I whispered into the dark. Jasper froze beside me.

"Me either," Jasper said after a short pause. Was I really considering offering to let him fuck me raw and fill me up? *I was.* Jasper groaned beside me.

"You ok?" I asked, worried at his random outburst.

"Yeah," Jasper chucked, his finger beginning to brush against me again.

"What will it take for you to feel comfortable with me filling you?" Jasper asked, his voice rough and low. *Was he nervous?* Fucking hell, the mental image of him filling me was doing something to my insides.

"Is there anything you need to feel comfortable?" I asked, avoiding his question, because my answer was; nothing.

"Ensuring with reasonable certainty that we aren't risking pregnancy," Jasper grumbled the words like the topic was hard for him to articulate.

"I'm pretty much in the same boat. I have a plan B at home," I whispered the last part, hopeful Jasper would get my drift. Jasper's hands flexed on my stomach, the only sign that he understood what I was laying down.

"You…" Jasper started, but was unable to find his words. I crawled out from under his hand, and over to his body. I leaned in close, the warmth of his chest radiating off him.

"I want you to fill me," I purred, punctuating each word with a slight pause.

"So mouthy," Jasper chuckled as his hands met my hips, his large palms flat and hot against my skin. Jasper pulled me the last couple of inches into his lap, my legs straddling his hips. I ground my arousal all over his straining cock. He was warm and hot underneath me.

"Ride me," Jasper commanded as his hips bucked slightly against me. I wrapped my fingers around his dick gently, lifting my hips off of his body and giving me enough space to guide the tip to my core. I paused, rubbing the pad of my thumb over the bead of pre-cum spilling from his tip. Jasper groaned, his head tipped back.

"Sparrow," Jasper begged as he thrust into my hand, his tip brushing against my pussy. I dropped down slightly letting the tip of his cock sink into my cunt. Jasper let out another low moan. I let go of his dick my hand landing on his chest to brace myself. I let the rest of my body drop down to his hips taking him in one go, right to the hilt.

"Fuck," Jasper groaned, his hands flexing on my hips.

"Good boy," I purred, rocking my hips over slowly.

"Ride. Me. Sparrow," Jasper gritted out. I smirked as I slowly rolled my hips again. Grounding myself with his shoulders, I lifted myself up and bounced on his hips once, and then twice. Jasper let out a low tortured moan as he thrust up to meet me. My arousal coated the underside of my thighs and the tops of his, as I rode his dick.

I kept riding him, chasing my own orgasm as Jasper encouraged from under me. My hips slammed down onto him as my pussy pulsed around him with my orgasm.

"Fuck," I moaned, as Jasper pinned my hips to his and he rutted into me. With his hands still on my hips, and his dick still deep in my cunt, Jasper flipped us over and my back hit the bed, Jasper's arms pressed into the bed beside my head.

"You sound so good," Jasper whispered in my ear as he slowly started to thrust back into me.

He took his time with each thrust, letting me feel the full length of his dick. Fuck I wanted him to go wild on me. I wanted to see him unravel. I snaked my arm out and up to his chest, running my hand up his chiseled body.

Wickedly, I wrapped my hands around his neck, not pressing hard, not choking him. I tapped my fingers against his pulse. Jasper's hand met mine against his neck, and he held my hand there as he started to thrust faster. Slowly, he pulled my hand from him and held it above my head, pressing my wrist into the bed.

"Come on, Cowboy," I egged him on, chuckling deeply.

"Brat," Jasper growled, his thrusts getting fast and sloppy as his control started to disappear into thin air. Jasper leaned down, his teeth nipping at my shoulder.

"Jasper," I gasped as a second orgasm rolled through my body, my legs wrapped around his hips and locked up, keeping him in place deep inside me. He gave me a moment to ride the high of my orgasm before he continued to rut into my cunt. *Fuckkk. He was a sex god.*

"Sparrow," Jasper groaned. Fuck he was such a vocal partner. He had groaned, moaned and grunted his own pleasure the whole time. *Such an ego boost.*

"Jasper. Fill me," I commanded. Jasper groaned at my words, his hips jerking slightly. Without breaking his rhythm, Jasper leaned over and flicked on the nightstand light.

"I want to see my cum spill out of you," Jasper groaned, his hands tightening on my hips. He had to keep his grip strong on my hips to stop my body from scooting away from him with each thrust.

"Fill me," I repeated. Jasper's face was blissed out as he chased his orgasm.

"Fill me," I chanted over and over again.

"Fuck, Sparrow," Jasper moaned as his cock jerked, before he slammed home one last time, spilling is seed deep inside me. He stayed still above me as his orgasm rolled through him. Jasper slumped slightly against me and pressed several light kisses to the side of my neck. Ever-so-slowly he thrust his still hard dick, fucking his cum deeper into me.

Jasper dropped his eyes down to where our bodies met. His eyes locked onto my cunt still swallowing his dick. He rocked back on his knees, pulling his dick from me and watching as his seed dripped down my pussy and over my ass and thighs. Jasper bit his lip groaning as he watched.

Only once every drop of his cum had pooled between my thighs, did he move again. In the soft quiet of the night, Jasper left and grabbed a warm cloth, cleaning me up. He took his time worshiping my body as he cleaned up his mess. I laid there, in his bed, my eyelids heavy with pleasure and sleep.

Jasper cleaned up the sheets with a towel before abandoning the soiled fabric on the floor, and pulled me close. He flicked the light off.

“Sleep well,” he whispered, pressing a soft kiss to my shoulder.

JASPER

The sharp trill of my alarm sung through my dark room. *Fuck.* It was so warm here, my mind groggy with the deepest sleep I had had in months. The gentle pressure of a warm body curled up next to mine. *Perfection.* I slipped my arm out from under Sparrow, who was sleeping through my alarm.

As my sleep filled brain woke up, the events of yesterday's evening came back to me. We had worshiped one another's body like faithful devotees. The night had been an emotional roller coaster: dinner with my family, then in Sparrow's apartment; leading to me running scared from her. Ending in her angrily knocking down my door, calling me out on my bullshit. Then falling asleep together after I made her cum six times.

I watched her sleep in my bed as I got dressed for work, having to change my jeans after discovering a hole in the crotch. I was down to my last pair of work jeans, this was the second pair this month that had ended up in the trash. Mentally, I added getting more clothes to my to-do list.

I padded down the stairs to the kitchen in my socks. I whipped together a quick breakfast and wrote a quick note to Sparrow, leaving it on top of her Doc Martin's that sat haphazardly by my door. I paused at the door, my hand resting on the door nob. *Fuck it.* Leaving my boots on the floor next to hers and my hat on the kitchen counter I bolted back upstairs.

I stepped back into my dark room and leaned down and kissed Sparrow on the forehead —she shifted and groaned. I inched back out the door glancing back through my door frame.

"Jasper?" her husky, sleepy voice called quietly.

"Go back to sleep, Sunflower. I'm headed out to work," I called quietly from the hall.

"No! Wait!" she stumbled from my bed and ran to me before throwing her arms around my neck. She nuzzled her face into my shoulders.

"Just the one night, Sunflower," I whispered into her warm hair.

"Is it sunrise?" Sparrow whispered back, sounding a little sad. Sunrise; the end of our one night.

"Don't be late for work," I whispered, winking at her before leaving her standing in my hallway *—smelling like me.*

"Wouldn't dream of it," Sparrow smirks at me before walking back into my room. I scooped my hat off the kitchen counter and pressed my feet into my boots, jogging to my truck. I tried to shove my heart back down into my chest where it had sat untouched for years, till Sparrow had shone a light on it.

My hand wrapped around the gearshift as I pulled away from my house and the woman who had touched parts of me that were starving for love. My fingers brushed the fabric that still sat wrapped around my gearshift. Having a small piece of her — a reminder of the happiness she now held— as a keepsake felt right. *No one else needed to know.*

The sun lit up the sky as I parked my truck, headed to the barn to pull Jackle from his stall and go to work. I was taking the trail out round the back of our land —having needed to check the back fields fences for damage. I took my time tacking him up, silently telling him about the woman who had out-shone the sun.

As Jackle and I left the barn, I watched Sparrow step out of her car, her dog following her at her heels. The little dog looked at her like she hung the moon and the stars just for him. *Me too buddy, me too.*

Jackle and I spent hours out on the land, looking out over the fields. Jett and I need to fix some of the fences out here before we brought the herd out here to graze on the wild flowers. And honestly, we needed to fence off a whole field, as half of it was now underwater. In the time since we had been up here last, a small lake had formed in the field. Jackle waded through the shallow water, cooling off.

It was the middle of the day and the sun beat down on us. Most of the wildlife had gone quiet in the sun, escaping underground or into the shade. I made note of the repairs needed and the specs for the new fence before joining Jackle in the lake.

The lake was shallow, the water clear —with wildlife springing to life around it. While the surrounding land around it had shriveled in the sun, the field around the lake was lush and bright with life. I left my boots in the mud of the lake shore and stepped into the cool water in my jeans, watching Jackle as he walked around in the water and nibbled at the grass under the water.

After splashing around in the water with Jackle for several minutes, we headed back to the ranch proper. We took the trip back slower, taking the time to look out over the land. I let out a piercing whistle as we passed by Caleb and Sam standing watch over the sheep; Jessie, our sheep dog resting in the shade of the fence, panting. *Happy as can be*. While technically, Jessie was Jett's dog, she had bonded herself to Caleb.

Sam waved at me as we trotted up to them; Caleb flipped me the bird with a cocky smirk. Jackle was sweet on Honeybee, Sam's mount.

"Where's Jett?" I asked as Jackle tried to reach Honeybee through the fence. She was not having it, ignoring him and her flicking tail out behind her.

"Out with Ked and the cows," Caleb threw his thumb over his shoulder. This year's calves had been rough, taking up more of Jett's time. He had spent more time in the last three months with the calves and our vet than the last year combined. It would cut into our profits this year, but the health of our cattle was the important part. Now, back in cell range I texted Jett all the information he needed about the fences before heading back to the barn.

Sparrow was marching around outside, her arms filled with hay and Salami running around at her heels. She was back in her black denim overalls, and looking goddamn amazing. She looked at me over her full arms and smiled, but kept walking away from me.

"Jasper!" Jett called round the corner I dragged my eyes from Sparrow to my brother. He frowned at me, his eyes darting to Sparrow's retreating form and then back to me.

"I think I found our girl, but there is a catch," Jett waved some papers in my face. I tried to listen to him talk about the mare he wanted to bring on, about how she would be an amazing breeding mare in a year or so. I just could not fully pull my mind from Sparrow.

This morning had felt amazing —my Little Sunflower had stolen my heart— but at the end of the day it was only supposed to be one night. *Did I even want more?* I wasn't really built for more; I was comfortable being single. *I liked my life as it was.*

Don't get me started on her connection to my family. What would happen with that connection when this exploded in our faces? My family would close in around me no matter her connection with them —I was blood. My mother would have my fucking skin for being with her to begin with. I could practically hear the words from her mouth. *She's twenty-two years old Jasper! What were you thinking?*

SPARROW

I lay in bed, hot and sticky. My skin was damp with sweat; my fingers slick with my need. I looked at the dark ceiling, my body soft in a post orgasm haze. I had been too horny to sleep, having replayed my night with Jasper in my head.

What were we doing? He was my boss and much older than me. . . not that the whole age thing bugged me. Jasper seemed bothered by the whole age thing; at least from how he was acting. *I'm not sure…* either way, he didn't like the age gap. I mean, it's not that big a gap —not like he was seventy and I was twenty. We were relatively in the same stage of life.

Maybe I was just rationalizing it because I was slightly addicted to him. I was so screwed. My self crafted orgasm took the edge off the heat boiling in my blood, enough to let my body fall asleep spread out naked on my bed.

Salami licked my face before my alarm could wake me up. I groaned into his ratty curls.

"I love you," I whispered to my soul dog. Salami cocked his head, his lips pulled back in what I dubbed his *'smile'*. My alarm trilled into my dark room. I swung my legs out of bed and turned my bed side lamp on —or at least I tried, but no matter how much I pulled the cord, it stayed dark. Groaning, I picked my way across my messy apartment. I was long overdue for a clean —my next day off. *I swear!*

The bright overhead light burned my dry eyes as I darted back towards my bed. I forgot to do laundry yesterday. *Fuck!* I pulled my overalls on from the dirty laundry and pulled on my last clean shirt. Rushing through my usual morning routine and clutching my red velvet latte in my hand as I ran out the door.

I was late, and Caleb stood outside the barn, arms crossed and tapping his foot.

"I'm here," I called, running towards him.

"I screwed up," Caleb blurted at me as I reached him. He looked terrified.

"What did you do?" I asked, sipping my coffee as we walked into the barn. Wordlessly he handed me his open phone. A text thread. In which Caleb had poured his heart out and had been left on read.

"Oh Caleb," I looked over at him smiling grimly.

"I know," Caleb pouted, taking his phone back.

"You are working with Jett today with the cows," Caleb mentioned before we parted ways and started work. I groaned internally —I had no doubt my day would be spent shoveling cow shit.

I was not wrong. Maybe it was good that I wasn't wearing clean clothes. Jett spent the whole day talking through his calving schedule for this month. The afternoon was much more enjoyable; I had spent the day chasing around a wild cow. The young cow needed to be taken to the vet over a misdiagnosed issue with its hoof. Not that it seemed to slow it down.

As Jett and I walked back to the barn covered in dirt and laughing as the cow had sent both of us to our ass multiple times, my phone buzzed in my back pocket. *Six messages waiting for me.* Three from Mama Harlow.

Mama H

Morning dear! We are having a family dinner tonight and it would be just peachy if you joined us tonight.

Mama H

Any dietary issues deary?

Mama H

I am adding you to the family group chat!

*#(***) ***-5541 was added to 'Harlow Clan'*

#(***) *** - 6987

Ma who you added this time?

Jasper

This is the family group chat…

The last message was from Caleb. Short and sweet only two words.

Caleb

HE replied.

We drinking?

Caleb

No! Tell you later!

I sent him a thumbs up before responding to Mama Harlow, confirming I would be there. I kicked my way into my apartment, greeting my eternal cheerleader.

"Walk?" I asked him as he ran around my feet in circles. I shoved a shit bag in my pocket and clipped his leash around my waist. Salami skipped down the stairs and around the edge of the building.

I pulled my phone from my pocket, debating on texting Jasper to warn him I would be at dinner. I had the message fully typed out as I rounded the corner to see Salami peeing on Jasper's truck —*again.*

"Rat!" Jasper growled at Salami. I was bent in half, laughing. I deleted the text as I snorted my way over to him. Salami finished peeing and looked up at Jasper, wagging his tail at the man.

"You sound like a dying pig," Jasper commented, smiling at me.

"Headed out?" Jasper asked, rocking in his boots, his hands shoved in the front pockets of his jeans.

"We are off out for a walk," I waved my hand out over the empty fields behind us.

"Can I join?" Jasper asked, sounding hopeful.

"Yeah," I said, starting to march on, Salami running around the two of us.

"You ever been out to the back fields?" Jasper asked, as we hopped a fence.

"Nope," I said, smiling at him. How would I get there? I couldn't walk all that way; it would take days, and there weren't any roads. I mean I guess I could ride a tractor or an excavator over there… but still.

"A pond has formed back there, and its beautiful," Jasper gushed, talking about the lake.

"I'm gonna see if Jett can help me fence it off and if we can keep it," Jasper explained his plan for the lake.

"That sounds great," I agreed. Something deep opened up in my chest as we walked through the field —whether it was part of me recognizing the land from when I was a child, or if my soul recognized the soul of the land, I did not know. But what I did know was that a missing part of me had healed here on Sparrow Road Ranch.

"I will take you up there any time," Jasper offered me, his face glowing from the late sun.

We circled back home, Jasper jumping back in his truck once we made it back —Salami forgiven or forgotten. I watched Jasper out of the corner of my eye as I climbed the stairs. He sat in his truck, looking out the passenger window, his fingers brushing over the gear shift before he pulled out and off towards his place. I jumped in the shower to wash today's dirt off of my body.

Salami sat outside the shower, his back to me, watching the door.

Once out of the shower, I plugged my hair-drier in and proceeded to dry my hair. I tugged at the strands trying to take a look at my roots growing in. I needed to touch up the blue in my hair. And thanks to Stackbooks, the internet had convinced me to add a couple black money pieces to frame my face. *Another day.*

With my hair dry, I started to style my hair. Once again, thanks to Stackbooks, I had found a new hair style I wanted to try out —these cute little heart shaped buns on the top of my head. I spent ten minutes fussing with little plastic hair ties till I was happy with the end result.

I wrapped the black fabric of my wrap-around skirt around my hips and tied the bow in the back; a lavender sleeveless turtle neck shirt on my top half. I pulled on a pair of matching lavender socks, the ribbon bows on the back of the socks similar to my skirt. They were a little longer than ankle socks, but not quite crew socks. To complete the look, I slipped my feet into a pair of black flats forgoing the boots today. *Sadly.*

Bribing Salami with his favorite treat as I left, darted to my car as fast as I could, hoping none of my co-workers spotted my outfit. I didn't need questions about where I was going right now. I argued with my car all the way over to the main house. She gave an ugly splattering noise as I pulled her to a stop. *That's not good.*

I still hadn't clarified in the *'Harlow Clan'* group chat who I was. Did they know I was coming or did Mama Harlow plan this behind their backs? I stepped through the door, opening my mouth to call out my arrival, when Mama Harlow came running from the kitchen, waving her hands at me.

"Shush dear," she hissed, pulling me into a hug.

"Go help yourself to a drink from the fridge," she said, releasing me. I quietly slid down the hall and around the corner into the kitchen and pulled open the fridge. The whole Harlow family was standing in the dining room, in full view of the open plan kitchen.

They didn't notice me till I popped open a can of beer, in which Papa Harlow started laughing his ass off—Mama Harlow joining in. Everyone looked up and over at me. I smiled and gave them a small wave.

"Surprise," Mama Harlow snickered, throwing her hands in the air.

"Sparrow," Jake called from his spot on the couch. I scuttled over and gave him a hug. The Harlow's took my arrival in step and went back to talking —Jasper smiled at me over his can of beer. *Why did he have to look so fine right now*. His eyes crinkled as he caught me eye fucking him.

"Ready!" Mama H called from the kitchen, and we all took a seat at the dinning room table. I sat next to Mama H, across from Jasper. Jasper kept passing me serving plates, smiling and asking each time if I wanted any, by simply stating what was on the plate. I filled my plate with hot comfort food. The conversation turned to the pond Jasper had found deep into their property. Jake was right on board with preserving the lake, but Jade had her doubts.

"You should get ducks," I blurted, into the conversation, every pair of eyes darting to me as I did so.

"It would be cool," I offered, panicking under their stares. I shoved another large mouthful of salad into my mouth, a drop of dressing rolling down my chin. Jasper's eyes tracked the dressing with a hunger that sparked.

"I love it," Mama H cooed, smiling at me. Jasper bit back his smile, taking his own bite of salad. I turned to Mama H and nodded at her, my hand coming up to wipe the dressing from my chin.

The evening came to a winding close as we all sipped warm drinks. I stood, stretching, before pulling the last of the dishes from the table and-starting to fill the sink, with hot soapy water.

"Sparrow, we are heading to the barn. Are you joining us?" Jett asked as everyone was pulling on coats.

"Yeah, I will be there in a minute, I'm just gonna do some of the dishes!" I called over my shoulder as I dropped the first round of plates in.

"Want help?" Jasper whispered in my ear softly.

"Sure," I smiled, tilting my head back slightly. Jasper stood next to me drying the dishes as I handed them to him. We talked quietly, well, *flirted* would be more apropo. Jasper's deep chuckle, mixed with my light giggle sounded like music to my ears. Jasper glanced over his shoulder before leaning down and brushing a light kiss to my cheek.

"Did you have fun?" Jasper asked. Even without a hint, I knew he was asking about the night we had spent together.

"Top five nights ever," I looked at him softly, a small smile pulling at my lips.

"Same," Jasper breathed, smiling back at me. As I finished up cleaning the last dish, I drained the sink and watched Jasper's forearms as he finished them.

"Thanks for the help!" I said, rising to my toes to brush my lips over his cheek, sneakily shoving my hand in his back pocket as I did so. I walked away, turning at the door and spending him a wink. Jasper just stood there, wet dish cloth in his hand, watching me. I left the room laughing as I darted from the front door and towards the barn.

As I ran past the house, and to my car, still laughing I could see Jasper through the large kitchen window looking down at a dark, small piece of fabric in his hand. *My panties.* Jasper was blushing and smiling at them in his hands.

Sparrow

Despite the high of flirting with Jasper at his family dinner, the rest of the week dragged on painfully. My room was still a mess by Sunday, and I was once again out of clothes. I shoved a load in my small unit washer, adding in probably twice the needed amount of scent beads into the load. My clothes *literally* smelled like cow shit.

I picked up the rest of my dirty clothes off of the floor and into a basket by the washer. I ran around with a large garbage bag picking out all the loose trash around the place and piled the dirty dishes in the sink, running hot water over them to start soaking. The first load in the washer was done, and I transferred it over to the drier and started the next load. I skipped into my small bathroom, sweeping all the products off of the counter and into a drawer. I sprayed cleaning solution all over the bathroom, letting it sit and do its work.

Next, I swept the floor and took the garbage and recycling out to the dumpster outside. I wiped down the bathroom and scrubbed the toilet. With my second cup of coffee for the day in my hand, I turned up the tunes and started to dance around my place, singing as I flipped my hair around and acting out the best super bowl half time show ever created.

I was a star! Salami barked and hopped around me, joining in as my back up dancer. After the brief reprieve, I settled back into cleaning and doing laundry. Afterward, as I took a much needed break laying down on my bed, the bread machine on the counter beeped at me and I dragged my tired body from my bed and pulled the pizza dough out. I stretched out three large pies, filling each one with different toppings and sliding it into the oven.

It wasn't long till I was chowing down on the first piping hot slice. *This is divine!* I packed up a few slices of each pizza, and hopped in my car. It wasn't long till I was knocking on Jasper's door with a box of pizza for him. Jasper tugged open the door "—can I call you back in five?" he spoke into the phone pressed to his ear. He hung up and stood in the doorway, looking down at me.

"You have to try this pizza I made…" I started to gush, handing him the box.

"This is what we are doing, now? This isn't a thing," Jasper frowned, his finger bouncing between him pointing at himself and then pointing at me, and then back to him again. I faltered; the box of pizza still outstretched in my hand.

"Oh right, I'm sorry I overstepped. I don't know what I was thinking," I apologized, pulling back from him. My hands dropped down, the box of pizza hitting my hip.

"Bye," I blurted, bolting from his doorstep. *Fucking asshole.*

I ran as tears spilled down my cheeks —I was pissed off at him. I tumbled into my room, no longer happy that it was spotless. Oh, of course I was the young ranch hand that fell for her older boss, and he wasn't into her. *I am so stupid!*

I screamed into my pillow, punching it. I slumped into bed, my tears damping the pillow.

I stayed there till I fell asleep, letting the darkness take over.

I kept my distance from Jasper for the next two weeks —which was hard, seeing as he was my direct boss right now. I was mostly successful. Caleb was being insufferable, as he had spent the last two weeks flirting through his phone. He had kept it to himself for two days, waiting till after to tell me about, how Felix had finally gotten back to him and that it was now going well. *Good for him.*

I was slightly ashamed to admit to myself that I had spent my lunch scrolling through my messages with Jasper, as Caleb giggled into his phone the whole time. I noticed how our messages started out professional, and then slowly, patches of flirting filled the thread, building up the more we talked —and then it all cut off, switching to radio silence.

It hurt.

Mama H

Family dinner tonight!

Wouldn't miss it!

This was going to be awkward as fuck. That evening, I stepped out of the shower and tugged on a tight pair of jeans —leaving me no temptation to wiggle free of my panties this time. I brushed through my wet hair, debating on the merits of just wearing a hoodie. Sighing, I settled on wearing my Swallow Road Ranch staff hoodie, and opted for my beloved Doc's. My wet hair cold in the night air as I dropped into my car and headed over to the main house.

I stepped into the kitchen, announcing my presence with a smile. I was welcomed warmly by everyone but Jasper, who watched me darkly over his beer. *Screw him.* Under Jasper's watchful eye, I mingled with his family, spending most of my time talking to Jade.

Dinner was served, but this time Jasper refused to hand me a single dish, even after I asked him to. He was sulking like a child over his own actions. *Ridiculous.* Once again, the Harlow's went for a walk after dinner, and I stayed behind to wash dishes. Jake paused on his way out, his eyes darting from me, to where Jasper stood, before he shuffled out of the room, and headed down the hall to his temporary bedroom. His body still healing from the car crash months ago.

"Sparrow?" Jasper asked, standing as far away as he could while still being in the same room as me.

"Yes?" I snapped a little more harshly than I intended.

"No need to be rude," Jasper frowned at me.

"See this is why we don't work," he hissed at me, his own temper flaring up. Panic gripped my lungs as memories of another night with a different man yelling at me echoed in my ears.

"Not that you even tried," I snapped back at him. Fighting had always been my response.

"Don't tell me what I did and did not do," Jasper snipped back. We went back and forth, poking at all the soft, weak places we had found in each other. We stood face to face, glaring at each other. I growled slightly, tossing the dish towel to the floor.

"Finish the dishes yourself," I stormed off. I felt like a child as I stormed away, leaving him alone in the kitchen.

This night was ruined. How did he make me feel so great and so miserable at the same time? I turned the key in my car, and it stalled. Slamming my hand down on the horn, I tried the key again. Nothing. *Fuck!*

Jasper came jogging out of the house at the sound of my horn and came over to my parked car.

"My car is done for," I whined, turning the key over again.

"I'll drive you home," Jasper pulled out his truck keys. The universe was being cruel this evening. I hopped into the passenger seat of the truck, refusing to look at Jasper. My eyes dropped to his hand on the gear shift as he parked in front of my place. His middle finger was tucked under a band of fabric wrapped around the gear shift. As his finger pulled off of the gear shift, the pattern of lace around the edge became clear to me. It was my panties… the original pair I had lost in his truck at the bar. *He still had those? And how did they get on the gearshift?* He stopped by the stairs leading up to my apartment.

"Sparrow," he called as I hopped out.

"I'm sorry," he apologized.

"I know," I smiled grimly at him before heading inside, not looking back. *He was confusing me.*

Salami greeted me with a whole body wiggle, back and forth as he crawled from the covers on my bed.

"You are the only man I can trust," I whispered to him. His wet tongue danced over my skin. Salami and I spent the rest of the evening cuddling. Not once did Salami question my quiet mood. The sight of Jasper's finger tucked into my panties that were wrapped around his gearshift was burned into my brain.

The next morning came far too quickly —Salami was still snuggling me in bed when I left for work. I stormed into the barn, a too-strong coffee in my hand and my hair swinging with attitude. I need to re-dye my hair soon —this evening seemed best.

Jasper was standing in the barn talking to Caleb as I approached. I walked past, them greeting Caleb with a silent pat on the shoulder as I passed, and completely ignored Jasper. I was tired of this jerking around — this hot and cold. *I was done with it!*

I sipped on my coffee as I started to fill the water troughs. Short of the horses, this places main livestock was the cows —both meat and dairy cows— and they had a small amount of pigs and sheep. I was not even gonna think about Mama H's personal chickens. *Chickens are evil.* Caleb walked past and whistled at me as I bent over the metal railing to fill another trough. I laughed at him as he walked away.

Jasper immediately came stomping over with a look of distaste on his face.

"He shouldn't do that; that is borderline sexual harassment!" he snipped, while also not being able to look away form my ass still hanging in the air.

"It's fine. He is a friend," I hopped down from the railing, the dust along the barn floor swirling at my feet. I walked up close to him looking up at him, under the brim of his hat.

"I want my panties back," I whispered in his ear before walking away.

I didn't have to look back to know he would be blushing under his hat. I almost made it out of the barn before he caught up with me.

"I only have the pair you gave me at dinner," he hissed at me, matching his stride with mine.

"I lost a pair in your truck as well. I want them back too," I hissed back, not looking at him. We walked side by side, neither looking at the other as we argued under our breaths.

"Then they are lost," he hissed back. Which I knew was *bullshit!* I had half a mind to tell him that, and I had my mouth open ready to do so.

"Come to my office in five minutes," Jasper whispered. I turned to snap at him.

"Unless you want me to hand them back to you out here with everyone watching," he said standing with his hands on his hips. Wait, he had them on him *right now. Fuck!*

"Office," I quipped before walking away. I waited a full ten minutes before heading over to his office —forcing him to wait for me. I skipped into his office a with large, sweet smile plastered over my face.

He was working on his computer, and without looking up he held up his hand, my panties from dinner hanging from his finger. I snatched the fabric from his hand, and as I did he looked up and smiled at me.

"Oh, Sunflower," he called as I turned to storm out of his office.

"Any time you want to loan out your panties again. I'd be happy to oblige," he smirked at me before turning his attention to his computer.

"I am mad at you," I snapped, before turning and walking away. The deep rumble of Jasper's laugh chased me down the hall. Was I mad or was I hurt? *Hurt.*

JASPER

Seeing Sparrow looking at me both mad and confused was adorable. She stormed out of my office with a swing in her hips. I didn't feel bad about lying and keeping the panties she left in my truck that first night. I couldn't quite let go of them; of her. *Not yet.*

I knew I had been a bit hot and cold with her, as my own emotions over our situation had haunted me. *I was confused too.* She was my addiction. I felt amazing when she was nearby, but like shit when she left. The withdrawal and slap in the face from reality was brutal. She brought something beautiful into my life; I felt so much lighter with her in my life. I had been living in the dark, and she was my sunrise. *My sunflower.*

But she wasn't mine. Not really. *Could she be?* I spent the rest of my day in the office, doing paperwork with Jake on the phone walking me through it. I fucking hated his filing system but since Jake would be taking back over by tax season, I needed to keep up with it and not tear the whole system down and rebuild it to my liking, like I would have preferred.

"Okay. I think I am done," I huffed, leaning back in the chair.

"Do you want a gold star?" Jake drawled sarcastically over the phone.

"Dick," I growled at him before hanging up. *Fucking asshole.* I pulled up my checklist on my phone, marking off *'paperwork'* from the top of the list. My eyes drifted down to the bottom of the list too *'Ducks'*. I smiled at the single word, being brought back to Sparrow's random suggestion.

I needed to get out of this office and dig my hands into the soil —reconnect with the land. Jackle greeted me with a soft nicker as I walked up to his stall. I tacked him up and left the barn. It was late afternoon and the sun was low in the sky. I let Jackle lead me where he wanted to go, and he walked slowly round some of the trails between the fields. Jackle was enjoying the peaceful afternoon just as much as me. We were on the same wavelength.

When Jackle stopped to munch on some wild flowers, I swung down from his back, looking out over the land. My house was just on the skyline, and behind it stood the main house. This land was a part of my blood, and my blood a part of the land. I stood there and let go of all my questions, giveing them to the land, feeling a new level of peace with its silent answers.

Soon, we started to head back. I walked beside Jackle, enjoying the feeling of the rough land under my boots. I needed this to clear my head. I had been so wrapped up in work, and the future of my family that I had lost what was important. I hadn't realized how much Jake's near death accident had been weighing on me. I had almost lost my brother — a key piece of my family, of me. A key part of this ranch. It was late, well past dinner, when Jackle and I made it back to the barn. I brushed him down and spoiled him with sugar cubes before bidding him goodnight and walking towards my truck.

A wild, carefree, laugh reached my ears. I turned my head towards the noise, and there was Sparrow. Laughing, her held tilted back, her cheeks flushed. She was standing in the parking lot alone, and was shining, her dress flying out from her hips. I stopped, watching her as her laughter built louder and louder. Her laugh turned into loud whopping calls before she tumbled into a fit of giggles. Her eyes shone bright, her cheeks bright red. *She was happy.*

This was my favorite Sparrow; the wild one. The one that looked like she was born to be a wildflower. *My sunflower.* Suddenly she stopped, facing me. We stood there watching one another, both frozen in place. Then, she turned and bolted away from the makeshift parking lot and towards the fields. She ran, her long legs eating up the ground. Her loose hair danced behind her as her skirt was dragged along for the ride, by her thighs. I took chase after her, fueled by the mischievous look in her eyes. As we barreled through the night, her laughter filled my ears again.

Sparrow let out a small shriek as she tumbled into a fence —she had tried to scramble over it and gotten stuck part way over. Now, she was half bent over the top, her ass in the air. I leaned against the fence beside her, looking at her through the wood.

"How you doing over there?" I asked, chuckling at her kicking her legs in an attempt to free herself.

"Screw you," she giggled. Seconds later like a switch was flipped she growled in frustration.

"Sparrow," I whispered deeply as she eventually freed herself from the fence.

"Don't," she warned, something glinting in her eyes.

"I am drunk," she pointed her finger at me in warning.

"We are done. I am done with this back and forth," she exclaimed, seeming to sober up a little as she aired her grievances with me.

"It hurts," she cut me off before I could open my mouth.

"I am worth more than that!" she screamed at me.

"I am not something convenient when you want me. I am a person with value, and feelings. And this on and off hook up thing we have going is not working for me anymore," she rambled. *Of course she had value! Where was this coming from?*

"I am done. I want more but I am not going to beg you for scraps of attention. I have more respect for myself than to give it up for a man I like, if he isn't going to give me the same in return. I may like you, but I have to walk away from this," she continued. I stood there, listening to the woman I was falling for, set her boundaries and draw a line in the sand. I had hurt her feelings —I had known that before— I just hadn't realized that by the time I had figured my shit out, it would be too late.

"Sparrow," I whispered again as she ended her tipsy tirade.

"What?" she snapped, frowning at me.

"I can't give you more right now," I admitted painfully.

"Then you need to walk away," she said numbly. I could see her eyes starting to fill with tears. *I just needed more time. I just needed to figure a few things out.* I couldn't promise her a future when I had no clue what mine looked like.

"From here on out, you are my boss, nothing more. Everything between us never happened," she snapped. She was burning with rage to hide the pain. As she stormed past me and into the night, I couldn't help but feel as though I had made the biggest mistake of my life as I watched the woman I was falling for walk away from me.

JASPER

It had felt like the darkest three days of my life—even worse than when we had been at each other's throats and pissed off. At least then she had been in my life; now she was just gone. Not even her blue and black hair disappearing around a corner. I had not seen her, heard from her, nor had anyone said her name in my presence.

Pratt

drinks?

Hell yes!

Pratt

8PM.

That was how, like many months ago, I found myself in Ernie's at eight waiting for Noah. *He* was late this time, and I had already started drinking.

"You look like shit," Noah greeted, sliding into our booth.

"Thanks, asshole," I growled at him. I wasn't much fun to be around these days.

"You ok, man? Like seriously?" Noah frowned at me, showing a level of concern I rarely saw from him. Not that he didn't care; it was more that he was always care free in his attitude.

"Yeah, I'm fine." I couldn't look at him though, so I stared down my whiskey.

"Bullshit. Mama H called me worried about you man," Noah said still with a seriousness my friend rarely needed to use. I looked up at him and didn't say anything.

"What happened?" Noah asked, leaving his beer untouched.

"Stuff. I don't know man, life's just kinda dark right now," I grumbled rubbing my jaw with my palm.

"I'll be ok, man. I appreciate the concern but it's just a rough patch. I'll be ok, I promise," I smiled at him —I had no clue in hell how I was gonna keep that promise, but I would find a way.

"Alright. I'm here for you, you know," he said, a little of his brightness returning, "you know, if you need someone to relentlessly mock you." And just like that we were back to the same old Noah and Jasper we had always been, drinking and generally being a menace to the world around us.

Noah recapped his past month to me, everything that had happened since I last saw him. An hour slipped by unnoticed as we joked about, buzzed from our drinks, before I noticed her. *Sparrow*. She was here. Dressed in a little black dress, her hair now a darker shade of blue. Her red Doc's were on her feet, and her long legs painted in fishnets. She was on the dance floor, a large pink cocktail in her hand and a group of men dancing with her. I watched her, entrapped. *My sunflower.*

At the end of the song, one of the guys dancing with her pulled her up to the bar and ordered her another, different cocktail, even though the one in her hand was only half finished. He took the pink one and left it on the bar, replacing it with a bright orange one. She leaned over and whispered in his ear.

Out of the corner of my eye I watched every single man in the bar try to flirt their way into Sparrow's pants. Each one bought her a drink she never got to finish before the next person swooped in and replaced it with something else. She was drunk. She floated and wobbled around the place, her face flush with the booze and excitement. Jealously screamed in my mind, her final words to me gluing me in place. *Everything between us never happened.*

Much to the enjoyment of the men around her Sparrow, started hitting on one of the other women at the bar. She was getting much farther with her flirting than any of the men had with her. She whispered into the woman's ear, who blushed and then leaned over and kissed Sparrow. The whole group of men watching them went wide eyed, and some even hollered and catcalled them. One guy let out a huge whistle.

Sparrow's eyes glowed as she slid a piece of paper with the woman's number into her bra, blowing her a kiss as she left. It was guaranteed that every man in a five foot radius was now hard. Not that I was any better. My dick had been fighting my jeans since I spotted her. The parallels from this night to that first night were uncanny and I couldn't push it from my mind. I had messed up badly. I knew that the instant that Sparrow and walked away the other night — now more than ever.

"See you tomorrow, man," Noah clapped me on the shoulder as he got up to leave.

"Tomorrow," I mumbled in agreement. His eyes flicked over to Sparrow before bouncing back to me, a question swimming in his eyes, and then he disappeared through the bar doors.

I got up, tossing the cash to close out my tab on the table. Most of the patrons had cleared out of the bar at this hour —they closed in an hour.

"Time to go," I informed Sparrow, who was giggling over the bar at something one of her love sick puppies had said.

"What?" she spluttered, looking up at me. Her eyes were shocked and confused, a little indignant too, but not mad. No hate burned in her eyes. That was almost worse than if she was furious with me.

"It's late. I will give you a ride home," I said softly.

"Do I get a snackie?" she asked, genuinely concerned. Great, she was in the toddler phase of being drunk.

"Yes," I promised, pulling her from the bar. She hadn't bought a single drink all night and had no tab to close, so I started to guide her outside. The cold night air brushed over us as I guided us to my truck. The fresh air seemed to sober her up some.

"Sparrow," I whispered, holding open her door for her.

"Don't *Sparrow* me!" she snapped, some of her fire for me coming back as she came back to her senses.

"Get in," I pushed.

"No," she argued, crossing her arms. I rolled my eyes at her.

"You are drunk; get in," I groaned, losing my cool.

"Policing my out of hours activities now, boss?" Sparrow snarled at me. The coldness of her voice jarring.

"You have work in four hours! You aren't even gonna be sober by then!" I snapped at her. She was the one who only wanted me to be her boss —so that was what I would be. She looked taken aback, shock painted over her mouth as it twitched. A single tear ran down her cheek, which she wiped away angrily, a cold mask settling over her face. She turned and gave me the cold shoulder before walking away from my truck and towards her car across the parking lot. How she got that thing working again was beyond me.

Before her mask could hide the pain I had caused, I spotted it, and as every spark of the wild woman I was falling for disappeared, something broke in me.

"Sparrow," I called softly. She stopped walking away and I caught up with her, mirroring that awful night where I had watched her leave me in the dust.

"What?" she snapped at me. I looked away from her cold eyes, the stars winking back at me as I looked up at them.

"Sparrow," I repeated.

"What?" she snipped louder this time.

"Please," I begged —for what I didn't know. *Mercy?* She frowned at me, the wheels in her mind spinning, working on the puzzle that was me.

"Give me a chance," I hoped.

"I gave you plenty!" she pointed out.

"Just one more," I pleaded, my eyes closed.

"No," she reenforced. I opened my eyes to her standing there with her arms crossed over her chest. Something burned in her eyes —burned brighter than the sun.

"Okay, Sunflower," I said, my sadness stealing my voice. I took a slow step back from her, never turning my back to her. As I slowly walked away —backwards— I drank her in as she stood there alone in the dark, the echo of her laughter having long faded into the night. As I got further away from her I could feel the light in my life slowly starting to dim. The sadness sat heavy in my chest. *Just an ember of hope.*

"Wait," she called so softly I almost did not catch it. We stood many feet apart our eyes locked across half the small parking lot.

"It would have to be the real thing, the whole thing. All of it," she said, her hands still hanging down limp at her side.

"No changing your mind in a day or two; you would have to stick with me. Give this a proper try," she outlined. I held my breath. Was she really giving me another chance? Light flickered in my chest.

"We would be dating. Exclusively. Something serious," she continued. *Right into the deep end —hell, I'd cliff dive for this woman.*

"How long is a proper try?" I asked roughly, which was not what I had meant to say.

"At least a month," she answered sadly. I stepped forward my strides getting more and more confident the closer I got to her. I looked down at her —still not having answered her.

"You get one last try, and it has to be serious. You have to mean it." She bit her lip, her eyes begging me to take this last chance.

"I will take all the time you give me, Sunflower. I won't need another chance. This is the only one I need," I whispered as I pulled her into my arms. I leaned down, dipping her back as my lips met hers. *Home.* She tasted like home.

"I promise," I whispered into her lips. She giggled and tipped her head back, deep into the dip.

"I think we should keep this between us —at least till we get on our feet," I whispered praying that I didn't just ruin my last chance. She frowned at me, doubt creeping in.

"Not for long. I just want to prove to you I am not wasting this chance before we add anyone else's thoughts and feelings to the mix," I explained, hoping it was enough.

"Not for long?" she asked. I nodded, leaning down to kiss her again.

"Does this mean you just asked me to be your boyfriend?" I chucked deeply. She laughed and pushed playfully at my chest, shaking her head.

"Do you want to be my boyfriend?" she asked, still laughing.

"Please will you do me the honour of being my girlfriend?" I asked as I spun her slowly across the ground.

"I'd love that," she hummed softly, her arms wrapped around my neck.

"Such a gentleman," she commented. smiling.

"You know what they say, 'a gentleman in the streets, a. . ." I started, till Sparrow slapped her hand over my mouth, laughing.

"I need to get back to Salami," Sparrow whispered after her laughter had died down, seeming shocked she had forgotten about him.

"Have you had dinner?" I asked abruptly. I didn't want to let go of her just yet.

"Yes," she answered, and my heart dipped slightly, "but I could use a dessert," she added, smiling at me.

"Dessert or *dessert*?" I asked, wiggling my eyebrows at her.

"The sweet kind —preferably with lots of chocolate," she giggled, shaking her head at me.

"I can do chocolatey. I'll drop you at home, and you'll come to my house in like half an hour?" I rested my forehead on hers.

"It's a date," she smiled at me. She felt so soft and relaxed under the blanket of the night sky. I kissed her one last time before letting her go. Once we were in my truck, she laid her head against the cold window, watching the road lit up by my headlights. The silence was comfortable; she had taken her boots off and tucked them under her body. I dropped her off at home, watching from my truck to make sure she made it in her door. I pulled away towards my home to make myself some food, and something chocolatey for Sparrow.

Sparrow

Jasper and I ended up pulling an all-nighter that night after the bar. I had brought Salami over with me, and we stayed up on the couch cuddling and watching movies. I had made one attempt to get into Jasper's pants about two minutes after I had walked in the door. Jasper had turned me down, claiming I was too drunk. *I totally was not!*

Work the next day had sucked. As predicted, I had not sobered up by the time I needed to leave for work, and on top of that I hadn't slept. Jasper had taken the easy route of doing paperwork in the office before he was joined by someone, and they took a couple horses out for a ride. I was stuck with a grumpy Caleb, and a mile long list of chores that were all labor intensive. It had been over twenty-four hours since I had been home by the time I made it back.

I had sobered up hours ago, and my hang over had dissipated before I had finished work. That had not been a smart choice, or had it? The night had ended up with Jasper as my boyfriend. I still expected him to panic over the whole thing and call it off in the next couple days, or the second he thought someone had found out. It had hurt when he suggested we keep our dating secret —I deserved to be loved loudly, not in shame behind closed doors. But I couldn't resist his pleading eyes.

I would give him the month I had made him promise to try for before I made a fuss over the secretive nature of our courtship. It was only fair. But after that, if he didn't want to love me in full view of the world, I would walk away. It would shatter my heart no doubt but I was not giving up pieces of myself to a man. *Not again. Never again.*

What did secretly dating Jasper even look like? He couldn't exactly spend a lot of time at my place — someone would recognize his voice through the wall. But was I supposed to go over to his house every time I wanted to see him? It wasn't like we could go out on dates. It would take five minutes till someone spotted us and recognized us. My phone buzzed with a notification.

Jasper

My place when you are done.

I drove home. I smiled at it, replying after I parked at home.

Boss or boyfriend?

Jasper

Boyfriend ;)

<3

I giggled at him as I walked up the steps to my home. Caleb was stumbling from his room in clean jeans and a dress shirt —tucked in no less.

His hair was still wet as he bolted from his place. He didn't even see me in his rush. I snickered to myself as I shot him a text.

No glove, no love!

Caleb

I don't know what you are talking about.

You almost just ran over me in your rush to get out! Nice shirt!

The three dots of Caleb typing popped up and disappeared several times before Caleb finally texted back.

Caleb

Thanks!

I fed Salami and took him out to pee. Jasper had gone out back to the bar in the middle of the day to get my car. I packed up a small overnight bag to bring with me, and then took the trek on foot, over to Jasper place. Salami ran around my feet and then ahead of me along the path we walked. Then he ran back to me, somehow managing to walk three times what I did. Jasper had left the door unlocked for me, and I walked right in. Or well, Salami ran in first like he owned the place. He ran over to greet Jasper, bouncing up at him. He threw his whole body into the air.

Jasper shooed him away, bribing him with a carrot. Salami ran away and curled up on the couch with his spoils.

"You know he does that 'cause he gets treats from you when he does," I said leaving my small bag hidden by my boots at the door. I settled down in a seat to watch Jasper cook and he flirted with me the whole time he cooked. This slow, domestic aspect of life felt amazing. It was a piece I was missing.

"Is that Mama H's lasagna recipe?" I asked as Jasper pulled the massive pasta dish out the oven.

"No, she won't share it with me," Jasper pouted, looking down at the dish.

"Darn if it was I was gonna bribe you into sharing it with me," I joked.

"Bribe how?" Jasper chuckled. I winked at him, sticking my tongue in my cheek suggestively. Jasper licked his lips, smirking at me.

"Naughty girl," he chided, smiling.

It wasn't long till a week had passed by and I hadn't spent a single night in my bed.

"Sorry, no sleep over tonight, Sunflower," Jasper informed me as he handed me a coffee. He had learned that bad news was best served to me with caffeine, especially this early in the morning.

"Family is coming over for dinner," he explained, kissing me on the lips. *Right, secret dating.*

"I know. I'm sorry," He whispered to my disappointed face.

"Jasper, it's okay. I never expected to be spending every night here," I reassured him. It was the truth, but why did it feel like a lie?

"But I like you here every night," Jasper replied. I wasn't sure if he was telling me, or himself.

"Me too," I sighed. We finished getting ready for work in silence, Jasper dropping me and Salami down the road from my place. I let Salami inside to feed him, then bounced down to my car. I drove back towards Jasper's place before turning off to go to the barn. *It would be so much easier if he could just drop me off at work.*

Jasper took every chance he got at work to flirt with me; a wink over his shoulder or a pointed look at me after someone made a sexual joke. Or when no one was around a soft lingering touch. Nothing scandalous, though I had tried to talk him into fucking me on the desk in the office at one point. He had seemed into it until he remembered it was in fact his brother's office and shut that down.

I tossed and turned all night long, unable to get comfortable in my bed. Salami slept tucked up against my neck. It was an hour before sunrise before I drifted off to sleep. Close to two hours later, my alarm woke me up again, and I rolled out of bed a zombie. A good morning text from Jasper was waiting for me.

Jasper

Morning Sunflower

Morning <3

I pushed my tired body through my morning routine. I added an extra shot of espresso to my coffee in hopes I would not kill my co-workers. I was putting a lot of pressure on a single shot of coffee, but it was all I had.

I pulled into my parking spot by the barn. Jasper was standing outside with several of my co-workers, Caleb's big smile was unnerving.

"Morning," I grumbled to the group.

"Morning, grumpy," Caleb joked, I glared at him as I took a sip of my coffee.

"What's up with you, Buttercup?" Travis asked, winking at me. I rolled my eyes at him, and peaked up at Jasper, who looked like he was trying not to laugh at him.

"Didn't sleep well," I grumbled.

"You can always crash in my bed. I'm sure you'd sleep great there," Travis offered. *Can I throat punch him?*

"I don't feel like catching a murder charge," I deadpanned, fluttering my eyelashes at him before flipping him the bird and walking away.

"Where you going?" Caleb called after me.

"Work," I hiked my thumb over my shoulder.

"Not so fast, *Buttercup,*" Caleb drawled, smirking at me at his use of Travis' nickname for me.

"We are working in the field today," Caleb pointed out over the land.

"Clearing a field," Travis added, smiling. *Great.* I resisted throwing my cup of coffee at him. *Can't waste good coffee like that.*

As we all made our way towards the field, Jasper settled in, walking beside me.

"Morning, *Buttercup,*" he smirked, as he whispered in my ear.

"Don't you start," I growled at him.

"Another coffee?" He offered, handing me one of the two mugs in his hand.

"Thank you," I whispered, taking the drink from him.

"I didn't sleep well either," Jasper admitted before increasing his pace to chat with the guys. I pulled out my phone and texted Jasper.

You are sooo close to losing pussy privileges!

I waited for my message to send, sipping the coffee he made me. I watched him as he pulled out his phone and looked at the text —and then almost spat out his coffee. I snorted before skipping past him.

"Have a drinking problem boss?" I jested as I flung my arm over Caleb shoulder.

"You lot give me a drinking problem," Jasper grumbled. My phone buzzed in my pocket. I waited a moment before pulling it out.

Jasper

Brat.

My eyes are up here. Stop staring at my ass ;)

Jasper looked at me, then slowly let his eyes drop down to my ass, smirking at me as he did so. *Asshole.* The day disappeared quickly as we got to work.

"Once you get this last section done, call it a day," Jasper called before he headed out early. My phone buzzed as I watched Jasper's muscled back, his shirt slick with sweat as he retreated.

Jasper

Come straight to my place after work (I will grab Salami)

Miss me?

Jasper

Of course, Sunflower.

It took us over an hour to clear the rest of the field.

"You busy tomorrow?" Caleb asked as we hiked back.

"Not particularly," I replied. Well, I mean I had plans to be with Jasper, but I couldn't say that.

"I need to run some errands, will you join me?" Caleb held the gate open for me.

"For a couple hours, sure," I wormed my way around the truth.

"Great!" Caleb exclaimed.

On my way! Btw I have plans to-morrow....

Jasper

Can't wait!

I pulled up to Jasper's house and parked my car around the side, keeping it from view. I skipped through the unlocked door. Salami wiggled his way over to me. After greeting me, Salami made his way back to his food bowl which was half full. I spotted a couple of Salami's toys around the room and his bed in the living room.

“I missed you, Sunflower,” Jasper pulled me into his arms, kissing my forehead.

“I missed you too. Did you bring Salami’s things here?” I asked, pointing to his bed.

“Yeah, that ok? I just thought he’d be more comfy,” Jasper shrugged.

“You didn’t have to do that,” I mumbled, fidgeting. Jasper looked at me, a complex look I could not pull apart flashed over his face.

“I feel gross,” I whined, pulling at my dirty shirt.

“Want to shower?” Jasper asked, smiling at me. I smirked at him and pulled off my shirt in the middle of his kitchen. Jasper groaned as he swooped over and picked me up into his arms. I wrapped my legs around his waist, rubbing my pussy against his cock, the rough fabric of my pants sliding over his jeans.

“Sunflower,” Jasper groaned as he ground his hard dick into my pussy.

Jasper consumed my mouth with his as he carried me upstairs to his shower. Jasper set me down on the sink, stepping back to look at my puffy lips and roughed up hair.

"Strip," Jasper commanded. I smiled at him as I slipped off the sink and turned my back on him. Holding his gaze in the mirror, I unclasped my bra, letting it drop to the floor. I slipped my jeans over my ass, watching his eyes fall down my body in the mirror.

My jeans hit the floor and Jasper reached out his hands, gripping my sides and hooking his fingers into the thin piece of red lace that hugged my hips. Jasper pulled my thong from my body, holding the small scrap of lace.

"I am keeping these," Jasper growled, leaning over me and dropping my thong into the sink.

"Get in the shower," Jasper smirked and slapped my ass gently with his hand.

Sparrow

I danced my way over to the shower and slipped behind the shower curtain. I stepped under the water, letting it soak my hair through. The curtain was pulled back as a naked Jasper joined me. Jasper stood there, outside the spray of the water. His eyes were dark and wide as he watched the water cascade over my body.

Jasper stood there, watching me under the water, his cock throbbing and at full mast as he took me in. I slowly turned around, my back to him, and I raised my arms above my head. I shifted gently from one foot to another, waving my ass at him. Jasper grunted from behind me right before I felt his hands land on my outer thighs. His large palms traveled up my thighs to my hips, and down to my ass. He gave my ass a tight squeeze. His fingers danced lightly over my back, over my shoulder blades and to my shoulders.

Jasper stepped closer, the front of his body pressing into mine. His cock pressed between my ass cheeks, his chiseled chest against my back. He placed soft kisses to the top of my shoulder as his hands looped round my ribs and brushed at the underside of my breasts.

He was soft and slow in the warm heat of the shower. His fingers cupped my breasts as his thumb brushed over my perky nipples. I could feel him thrusting lightly against my ass as I ground my hips into him in a slow circle.

Jasper dropped his hands from my tits as he picked up a bottle of shampoo, rubbing the clear soap in his hands before gently massaging it into my hair. Once he was happy with his work he moved on to his own hair, rubbing the leftover shampoo into his hair.

He continued with the conditioner next, and then on to body wash, each time starting with me and then using leftover product on himself. Once we were both clean, I resumed my grinding against his dick, pulling a low groan from his lips.

"Sunflower," Jasper warned, his hands on my hips.

"Yes?" I asked coyly, turning my head to look up at him over my shoulder. I rubbed my ass against his dick one last time before pulling my body away from his. Jasper and I stood half in and half out of the water.

"Jasper," I called softy, before reaching down and wrapping my fingers around his balls, giving them a gentle tug. Jasper let out a gasp and then a deep moan, his eyes flickering shut. I quickly sank to my knees before him. I grasped the base of his cock, before licking the water off of it. I looked up to find Jasper's flushed face looking down at me with hooded eyes.

I smiled up at him before licking the tip of his dick in one long stroke of my tongue. I opened my mouth, taking him in. Several inches of him comfortably sat in my mouth. I pressed my tongue into the underside of his cock before I gave him a generous suck. Jasper cursed above me, his fist slamming into the wall to steady himself.

I wrapped my fingers around the base of his cock as I started to suck on him letting him, slide in and out of my mouth. Slowly, I took more and more of his cock into my mouth. Jasper slowly started to thrust into my mouth in rhythm with my sucking. I hollowed out my cheeks, the wet sucking sounds from my lips starting to compete with the sound of the shower.

"Sunflower," Jasper grunted in warning. I picked up my speed, wanting him to spill into my mouth.

"Sparrow," Jasper barked out in warning again. I could hear his panting above me. Jasper's hand landed on the top of my head, pressing gently into me as he pulled his cock from my mouth. I sat there on my knees before him, as he stood in front of me, both of us panting. His thick pink cock bobbed right in front of me, looking hot and heavy and needy.

I reached out to take him back in my mouth, again.

"Wait," Jasper breathed, pausing my movement. I looked up at him as he closed his eyes for a moment before opening them again and looking down at me.

"I want to fuck you," Jasper grumbled. He helped me to stand as all the blood rushed back into my legs. He cradled me against his body till the feeling came back to my legs. Once I no longer resembled a new born horse, Jasper dropped his hand down onto my body, past my breasts and to my pussy.

Jasper's fingers brushed over my clit, before sinking into the wet folds of my core. Slowly, he finger fucked me with a single digit. I leaned forward, pressing my ass into Jasper's dick. I was bent in half in front of Jasper as he added another finger to my pussy.

"Who does this cunt belong to?" Jasper asked in my ear as he used a third finger to circle my clit. He was slow and deliberate with his movements.

"Me," I gritted, defiantly. Jasper tutted behind me, pulling his fingers from my pussy. I could hear the sound of Jasper licking my arousal from his fingers right behind my ear. I whined, protesting the absence of his fingers. I reached down and started to rub at my clit, seeking relief myself.

"Nuh—uh, naughty brat," Jasper chided, pulling my hand from my pussy.

"Who does this cunt belong to?" Jasper asked again, holding my hands in his. I could feel Jasper press his cock into my ass.

"You," I moaned at the press of his hot cock.

"Good brat," Jasper purred in my ear as his fingers dropped to my pussy again, sliding three fingers into me. As he thrust his fingers into my pussy, and his dick into my ass checks, he guided me over to the edge of the shower. He bent me over the side of the shower, with my feet planted wide outside the stream of the shower.

Supported by the side of the shower and my weight folded over, Jasper removed his fingers from me and sneaked his hand around to the back of me. His fingers pressed into me again from behind. He gave my pussy a couple good thrusts as his other hand pinched at my ass.

"Fuck, you look so good bent over for me," Jasper groaned as his fingers brushed over my clit as he pulled them from me. Jasper's fingers then wrapped around his cock as he spread my arousal from his fingers onto himself, before guiding his cock to my pussy, and pressing the head of his cock into me.

I let him work himself into me, resisting the urge to press myself back into him in case I lost my balance. Once Jasper was seated to the hilt inside me, he wrapped his hands around my hips before slowly pulling me closer.

"You take me so well," Jasper groaned. Jasper started to thrust into me in strong powerful thrusts. He kept up his slow, relentless pace with long powerful thrusts as he almost completely pulled out of me before slamming back into me again.

It wasn't long till I was a boneless mess in his hands, babbling, and encouraging him on as I steamed straight towards my second orgasm. Jasper continued at his pace, making sure we didn't risk a fall. He started to pick up speed as his thrusts became sloppy and it wasn't long until my pussy spasmed around his cock as another orgasm rocked my body. He knew how to treat my pussy just how I liked it.

"Fill me," I moaned as Jasper got closer and closer to his orgasm.

“Fuck, Sparrow,” Jasper groaned, as he spilled deep inside me. He started to thrust into me again, fucking his cum deeper into me before he pulled out. Jasper pulled me upright and into the stream of the hot water, gently cleaning his seed from my body and then flicked the shower off and stepped out of the shower. He grabbed my towel and wrapped me up, as he dripped into the bath met, before grabbing his own towel.

Sparrow

I darted to my house and hopped in the shower, washing the day away. I braided my still wet hair and brushed some blue mascara on my lashes. I pulled on a cute sage green matching set of panties and bralette, sticking my legs into a fresh pair of black denim overalls. The temperature had dropped today, so I pulled on my black crew-neck sweater with '*Go to Hell*' written in navy on the back.

I clipped the overalls and grabbed my purse, slinging the backpack style purse onto my back. I kissed Salami goodbye before dancing down the stairs to Caleb's waiting car. I slipped into the passenger seat as my phone buzzed.

"Hello," I greeted as Caleb pulled out. I peaked at my phone; it was a text from Jasper.

Jasper

Enjoy your afternoon! See you later ;)

"Who are you texting?" Caleb asked, trying to sound innocent. I looked up at him and he was trying to hold back a smirk.

"Nosy," I jested.

"Bitch! Spill," Caleb demanded as he pulled onto the highway.

"I don't know what you are talking about," I slid my phone away from his eyes.

"Sparrow! I know you are seeing someone!" Caleb exclaimed.

"I am, and?" I pressed, raising my eyebrows at him.

"So spill," Caleb egged on.

"How is Felix?" I asked, avoiding his request.

"I don't know, you would have to ask him," Caleb said, not looking at me, his face bright red.

"What is going on between you guys?" I pressed, hoping to avoid talking about my relationship.

"Its complicated," Caleb whispered.

"So talk me through it," I offered. Caleb spent the rest of the drive talking through his non-relationship relationship. How they had gone on one date that had gone well and ended in a mind-blowing kiss. Then hearing nothing for weeks, till they had ended up at the same house party, where they hooked up in the bathroom. They had been talking and flirting back-and-forth for weeks since, but nothing had come of it.

"Was his dick really that good?" I asked as we pulled into the mall parking lot.

"Yes," Caleb confirmed. We chatted as I followed Caleb around the mall, running all of his errands.

"Want to shop for a bit?" Caleb offered as I stared into the display window of a store.

"Yeah," I mumbled as I dipped into the store. My phone buzzed in my pocket with an in-coming call from my cousin, *Daisy-Mae* .

"Hello," I greeted, picking up the call. Daisy's side of the family and mine did not get along, except for a few of us. Daisy's mother was my fathers half sister. My family, however, refused to talk to any of *those Kingley's.*

"So, I don't have your new address so I can't send you the invite, but. . ." Daisy drew out the *'but'*.

"You are invited to my wedding!" Daisy bubbled at me. The two of us giggled over the excitement for the coming wedding and Daisy promised to send me all the details over email before hanging up.

Caleb and I shopped around, picking up new clothes for the both of us for another half an hour.

"I gotta head out soon," I pointed out as we left the last store.

"One last stop," Caleb said, blushing as he pulled me into a Luster's store, filled with gag gifts, merchandise for popular shows, and the back half of the store was full of sex toys. Caleb kept his hand linked with mine as he pulled me to the back of the store.

"Caleb," I hissed, trying not to laugh.

"Shut up," Caleb snapped, blushing. I stood with Caleb as he awkwardly fumbled through the different pairs of handcuffs. Settling on a simple leather pair, Caleb rushed to the checkout without me. I snooped through all the lingerie hanging on the wall. A sexy cowgirl set caught my eye —the look on Jasper's face if I turned up in that. I found a navy lace teddy that caught my eye, and I picked it out and grabbed the cowgirl set alongside it.

With my lingerie paid for and in a black bag, I joined Caleb outside the store, who glanced at my bag.

"That for the person you are seeing?" Caleb asked, trying to be subtle.

"Who said I was seeing anyone?" I asked as we walked to his car.

"You! I know you are seeing someone! You haven't been home all week," Caleb pinned me down with his eyes.

"Fine. I am secretly dating someone," I whispered, blushing.

"Who?" Caleb squeaked.

"Secret dating," I rolled my eyes at him.

"Dump them," he demanded.

"Why?" I whined as we got back on the road towards home.

"You deserve to be loved loudly," Caleb said, his eyes on the road.

"So do you," I pointed out. Caleb waved me off.

"She or he?" Caleb asked. I spluttered at him. I hadn't told anyone that I was bisexual, and while I knew telling Caleb would be fine as he himself was openly gay, I just hadn't settled in enough at the ranch to tell anyone —well any one other than Jasper. Who had learned it via my dating history.

"I know your last ex was a chick," Caleb shrugged. *Chris.* She had been amazing. We didn't get the chance to get super serious in the three months we had been seeing each other before she had moved for work.

"He," I conceded.

"So why is he keeping a you secret?" Caleb asked.

"Who said he was the one who was keeping me a secret?" I asked, avoiding his question.

"You love loudly, and don't strike me as someone who cares what people think of their relationship," Caleb answered.

"Fine, yes he has his reasons, good reasons. I totally get it," I finally responded.

"And I am giving him a month to deal with it and tell people or I am walking away," I added quietly.

"Good girl," Caleb praised. Caleb parked back in the parking lot at home and we both juggled our way back into our respective apartments.

"Enjoy your night," Caleb winked as he walked into his place. Salami wiggled over to me when I walked in the front door, his plastic travel bowl of water sitting where his ceramic bowls used to sit. His ceramic bowls now were sitting in Jasper's kitchen.

I sorted through the bags of stuff I had bought. A couple new books that I placed on my bookshelf, the missing cleaning supplies, more hooks to hang things on the walls, a refill of my favorite sunscreen, new first aid kit, more work clothes, a new toy for Salami and of course, my new lingerie. Salami was carrying around his new stuffed hedge hog toy in his mouth, his lips pulled up into a doggy smile around the toy.

I packed up another bag of my things to bring to Jasper's and Salami's new toy and headed over to his place. Jasper's door was locked when I got there. I knocked on his door and waited a moment before calling him.

"Hey, Sunflower," he greeted, the distant sound of his video game filtering through the phone.

"I'm here," I sigh.

"I'm coming," Jasper said, unmuting his mic and bidding the other players goodbye, keeping me on the phone as he ran to the front door. The door swung open and I hung up the call. Jasper stood in the doorway wearing only Joe boxer lounge pants that hung low on his hips. I was practically drooling over him in the door way. Jasper stepped aside to let me in. Salami had already let himself in and was curled up on the couch already.

"I missed you, Sunflower." Jasper pulled me close, his mouth seeking mine.

"How was your evening?" I asked as he pulled me towards his bedroom.

"Good. Would have been better with you, but it was nice to hang out and play with the guys," Jasper settled down on the bed.

"Cuddles?" Jasper asked, pulling me into his lap.

"Absolutely," I whispered leaning into his chest. *This felt so good.*

"I was invited to a wedding," I whispered into the quiet room.

"How fun," Jasper commented.

"Want to be my date?" I asked, biting my lip. Jasper tipped my head up with one finger hooked under my chin. He looked down into my eyes for several moments.

"I'd love to," he replied.

"What should I wear?" Jasper asked against my ear.

"Clothing, probably a suit," I giggled.

"Not what I meant. I meant what are you wearing so I can match," Jasper chuckled.

"Blue," I responded rolling my eyes and waving at my hair.

"Okay, Sunflower," Jasper rumbled deeply. His lips found my shoulder, trailing soft kisses over my skin.

"Bed time," Jasper said, pulling me down into the bed. Jasper unclipped the straps of my overalls. His hand slid up the back of my sweatshirt, searching for my bra strap. He paused as his hand skimmed over the soft back of the bralette.

Without a word and with fire burning in his eyes, Jasper pulled my shirt over my head, his eyes drinking in my skin.

"The bottoms match," I whispered in his ear.

Jasper's fingers fumbled as he undid the rest of my overalls, peeling them off of my body. He looked down at the matching g-string with the hunger of a starved man. Jasper leaned down, his hands rubbing over my hips. He placed kisses along the waistband of the panties. Then his lips dipped down and over my hip, his lips meeting the soft flesh of my ass. Groaning as he was bent over me, I laid out on my stomach to give him access. Jasper's teeth nipped at the soft flesh of my ass.

"Stunning," Jasper praised as he nibbled back up to the green fabric.

"Radiant," Jasper mumbled as he tugged at my g-string with his teeth.

JASPER

My Sunflower was laid out on my bed, her ass in the air, the scrap of fabric on her ass teasing me. *Fuck, she is so perfect.* I bent down to kiss the round mound of her ass, kneading the muscle in my hand.

Working on the ranch these past months had toned her body even more than it had been when we met. Despite her muscles, she remained soft, her gentle curves filling out her clothes. I was a goner for this woman. I nibbled at the fabric around her waist, using my teeth to pull the g-string off her body.

Once I got the fabric of her panties over the swell of her ass with my teeth, I grabbed them and tugged them down her body. I drank in her body, the bare skin, the little scars that flecked her body.

She was on her hands and knees, her ass in the air for me, her legs slightly splayed under her. I trailed my hand over her ass, down the start of her thigh and to her pussy. I brushed a single finger over her cunt lightly. I watched the shiver roll through Sparrow's body. She was soaking wet for me. *Fuck.*

"You look so good for me, Sunflower," I purred, looking at the gleam of her arousal on my finger and the lips of her pussy. Sparrow tilted her hips up, creating more space for me to see her.

"Such a greedy cunt," I purred as I lowered my body to meet hers. I ran my nose up the back of her thigh, pausing before her pussy. I let my warm breath fan out over her needy skin. I licked with a wide flat tongue over her. I closed my mouth over her pussy and sucked gently. Alternating between thrusting my tongue as deep as I could into her pussy and sucking on her clit, I could feel the little tremors wracking Sparrow's body as she climbed closer and closer to orgasm.

I kept up my slow, teasing pace, using my tongue to bring her pleasure. My only goal was to bring her trembling to her proverbial knees with pleasure. I wanted her bordering on over-stimulated with orgasms before I fucked her with my cock. I reached down between my thighs as I continued to tease her first orgasm from her body. I fisted my cock in my hand, holding the hot flesh in a firm grip. My other hand gripped her thigh. Sparrow was loud with her encouragement for my tongue.

I teased two more orgasms from Sparrow, who was now a trembling mess slumped over my pillows. I had resisted fucking my hand while I ate her out, but now she would be getting my cock, which she had spent the last orgasm begging for.

"Ready?" I asked, pressing the head of my cock to her messy cunt. Sparrow whined her consent as she pressed her hips back against my cock. Sparrow spread her pussy over my cock till it reached the hilt, her ass pressed into my hips. I let out a grunt as the wet warmth of her cunt gripped my cock.

Sparrow looked over her shoulder at me, her eyes bright with pleasure. Sparrow was relaxed and orgasm high, and looked so hot. I was not gonna last long like this. I rubbed my hand over my face, some of her arousal still coating my chin.

I thrust into her slowly as she eagerly met each one with her hips. I gripped her hips tightly trying to slow her down so I lasted longer. She felt *so* good. Sparrow grumbled under me. I pulled back, ignoring her protests. With her hips in my hands I flipped her over onto her back. My greedy brat smiled up at me, her face flushed.

I loved the sight of her blue hair spread out over my bed. I didn't leave her disappointed for long before I once again buried my cock deep in her hot cunt. I placed my hand on the mound of her pussy, my thumb seeking out her clit as I thrust into her. I circled her clit in rhythm with my thrusts. As predicted, I did not last long and it wasn't long before my body took over as my orgasm curled around my balls and rocked through my hips. I thrust into her one last time emptying my balls deep inside her. As my seed spilled into her, she tipped over the edge of her own orgasm, her pussy pulsing around my spent cock, milking the last of my cum from my cock. I boarded on overstimulated by the feel of her orgasm around my cock.

SPARROW

Jasper and I planned to make my cousin's wedding a full weekend trip. The week of, I drove up a day early on the Thursday. I had booked the time off since it was a family wedding. Jasper would join me Friday evening. I handed Salami over to Caleb for the weekend, as I could not find a single pet friendly hotel in the area, and I stopped by Jasper's to pick up the bag I had packed for the trip.

Jasper had my dress hanging in the back of his truck that he was gonna drive up, as my car did not have the space.

"Wait, before you leave," Jasper pulled me in for one last kiss.

"You will see me tomorrow evening," I chuckled.

"For you," Jasper grabbed two boxes he had hidden on a chair. I took the much larger box from him, ripping the baby blue wrapping paper off of the box.

Under some pale blue tissue paper there was a pair of white Doc Martin boots. I lifted it up. On the back of them sat a small yellow charm; a sunflower.

"To wear at the wedding," Jasper elaborated. He then handed me the smaller box. I peeled the paper back to reveal a small jewelry box. Inside were matching sunflower earrings.

"You didn't have to..." I said, tears springing to my eyes as I looked at the small gem stones that made up the earrings.

"You deserve it and I wanted to," Jasper whispered before kissing my check and sending me off for the day.

It was a good four hour drive to where Daisy-Mae was having her wedding. I stopped in a small town an hour from my destination for lunch. I walked town the main street looking for somewhere to eat when I ran into a small farmers market. I slipped into the crowd of people browsing each table. The variety of craftsmanship at each stand was mind blowing. I picked up several handpies for the road and a raspberry lemonade. I was about to leave, when I stopped at the stall of a local silver smith. My eyes landed on a silver band, a small round yellow jewel set in the center. *It was perfect.*

Then I found what I didn't know I had been looking for. A stunning pair of silver cuff links winked at me. With the same yellow jewel; they were sunflower cuff links. With my surprise for Jasper all wrapped up, I headed back to my car. The rest of the drive flew by as I pulled into the hotel parking lot.

I found our room and checked in, leaving my overnight bag behind in the room. *I missed Salami.* I pulled out my phone and called Daisy, letting her know I got to the hotel safe and sound.

"That's great, why don't you freshen up or eat and then head over here," Daisy bubbled. There was no other way to describe her way of speaking. Daisy was a blue eyed, blonde haired beauty queen. Her soon-to-be husband was a hunter and fisherman; that was all I knew about him.

I vaguely remembered seeing their engagement announcement post months ago.

"Be there soon," I said before hanging up. I spent the rest of the day with my cousin, having a fun spa day and doing our nails while getting tipsy. It was late when I got back to the hotel and curled up in the big bed, dressed in Jasper's shirt—that he didn't know I'd taken. I called him, hoping that he wasn't asleep yet.

"Sunflower," his groggy voice greeted.

"Did I wake you?" I asked quietly.

"No," Jasper yawned. I fell asleep with Jasper still on the line, waking up early without my alarm to the phone call still open, Jasper snoring on the other end.

The wedding was tomorrow, but first, I had Daisy's bachelorette party to go to this afternoon. After arriving, I huddled in the corner, feeling a little like an ugly duckling. Daisy's party was in full swing—we had been limited to two drinks per person, and they were all sparkling wine spritzers or white claws. I was in a sea of natural hair colours, my black and blue dyed hair standing out. I was bored, but this was the party Daisy wanted. So it was the party she got.

Jasper texted me saying that he was just hitting the road. In just under four hours, I would be in his arms. That thought kept me going through the rest of the party. After leaving the party at six, I curled up in the hotel bed with a large serving of hot fudge brownie with ice cream. I fell asleep soon after finishing my sweet treat and was woken up with a start by the ringing of my phone.

"Yes?" I answered groggily.

"I am down the road, Sunflower," Jasper's deep voice crackled over the phone. *He is here.* I sat up in bed wide awake. Minutes later I was opening the door for my cowboy. Jasper sauntered into the room, his overnight bag over one arm and the bags with our clothes for tomorrow over the other.

"I missed you. Sunflower," Jasper whispered, his lips brushing mine. Jasper's scent flooded my nose.

"I missed you, too," I hummed into his mouth.

"I got you a surprise," I whispered to him, handing over the box.

"Sparrow," Jasper hummed taking the box. He pulled the box open and took in the cuff links.

"I love them," Jasper thanked, looking up at me. He pulled me into his arms and kissed my hair. He rocked us back and forth slowly for several moments.

It wasn't long till Jasper and I were cuddled up under the bed covers, naked. His fingers traced patterns over my skin as we drifted off to sleep. It wasn't long till our month was over, and my stomach pinched at the thought. *Would this last? Was he serious about this? Would this be the end of us? Would I walk away? Would he? Would he tell people? Only time would tell.*

Jasper had opted for a light gray suit with a navy shirt and pocket square; and of course the cuff links I got him. My navy dress matched his shirt perfectly, my new Doc Martins on my feet. It was one hell of a way to break them in. The matching earrings shining in my ears, we looked quite the pair.

"Not my favorite type of wedding," Jasper whispered as we walked into the huge vaulted-ceiling barn.

"Right?" I giggled, taking in the huge floral arrangements around the place. A dance floor and bar had been set up in the back with a section of large tables to the right and a perfectly rustic aisle way down the middle. I'm pretty sure Daisy's father paid a pretty penny for the hand weathered wooden frame standing in the middle of the room. Jasper and I took our seats and waited for the wedding to start. The ceremony was beautiful, and I had in fact cried at their vows. Jasper had cried too.

Their music choices had been amazing, such that most guests spent the evening dancing. Jasper had spun and swirled me around the dance floor all night. It wasn't until half the guests had left and only a few of us were still on the dance floor, that the music had slowed down. I swayed in Jasper's arms, my head resting on his shoulder.

"What is your dream wedding?" Jasper asked quietly. I leaned back and looked up at him.

"Not this," I giggled.

"Something small, definitely outdoors," I elaborated after a moment. Jasper hummed at my response.

"You?" I asked.

"I didn't think I would ever get married," Jasper commented.

"Do you still think that?" I asked, some emotion choking my throat.

"No," Jasper admitted. *Did he just admit his view on marriage changed? Did we just discuss and agree on our stance on marriage?* My head rested on Jasper's chest, his heartbeat thundering in my ear. Neither of us spoke again for a while.

"Shall we head out?" Jasper asked, spinning me in his arms.

"Sounds good," I hummed. We floated from the dance floor as the song ended. I scooped up my boots from the edge of the dance floor where I had abandoned them hours ago.

"Wait!" Daisy called, running after us through the crowd of people. She was bare foot like me, and had her dress hiked up to her knees as she ran towards us.

"I have a gift for you," she panted, standing in front of us. Daisy dragged us to a small room down the hall on the way to the door. She came back out holding her bouquet. Smiling, she handed it to me. My mind went blank as the flowers sat in my hand. *What?*

"I have a feeling," Daisy whispered her cheeks glowing pink. I watched as she skipped back to her party and her new husband.

"Did she just. . . " Jasper said, his words dropping from his mouth as he watched her leave us.

"Yup," I said, turning and pushing towards the door.

Jasper

Sparrow had settled into a routine with me, staying at my place every night. I swear she was half moved in already, not that I was complaining. My once clean, orderly house was tossed into chaos, clothes everywhere in my bedroom, makeup and several different soap products all over my bathroom and dog toys all over my living room. Several of her mugs in my kitchen, and a whole coffee shop's worth of coffee syrups on the counter.

My Sunflower had grown all over my life and I was all for it. I was wrapped around her pinky finger.

"I got invited to family dinner again. . ." Sparrow called as she walked into the room, her eyes locked on her screen. She looked up at me, waiting. My month was up yesterday, and while she hadn't said anything, I knew my time was up. She wanted serious, she wanted the whole deal and that meant telling people. I had been avoiding this enjoying our secret little bubble.

"I know. I know. I am planning on telling everyone, I just need a little more time," I pleaded. Sparrow huffed but gave in.

"Probably not a good topic for family dinner," she conceded.

"I promise, soon," I wrapped her in my arms. I had worked today, but it had been her day off and it had been the longest day of my week.

"We don't need to leave for another hour," I whispered in her ear. She hummed, leaning into my body.

"Nap?" I asked, my body bone tired. Sparrow didn't answer, but started to head towards our bedroom, pulling me after her.

Curled up in my arms, and her body pressed to my chest, we both fell asleep quickly, the hour long nap feeling like mere minutes. Sparrow scrambled to get ready so that she could swing by her apartment before going to dinner.

"Sparrow," I called as she tugged on her boots. I pulled her close, slipping my hand into her back pocket. I leaned down kissing her, savoring her lips as it would be my last for several hours.

"I love you," I whispered quietly, partly hoping she wouldn't hear me. I just needed the universe and the land to know the truth.

"I love you, too," she whispered back before her lips met mine again. Then she was out the door and into the night. I shouldn't have told her that right before dinner. *I just made dinner harder.*

I grumbled my way into the main house where Ma was cooking dinner and Jade was cuddling her baby and talking to her.

"Jasper," Ma greeted, hugging me. My chest felt heavy knowing I was keeping a huge piece of my life from her.

"Beer?" Pa asked, holding the fridge open.

"Whiskey," I muttered before kissing Jade's baby on her head. Jade looked pale and stressed and her conversation with Ma was swept under the rug now that I was here.

Pa slid a glass of whiskey and ice towards me. I nodded and took a sip of the dark liquor. The door opened and the familiar mango scent of

Sparrow hit my nose. I tipped the glass, taking down the whiskey like air. I finished my glass as Sparrow walked into the kitchen. The woman I loved smiled at my family and was greeted warmly by everyone.

I was so screwed. It wasn't long till we were all seated around the table and I was fidgeting as I tried not to look at Sparrow or give away my feelings. After dinner Sparrow was roped into helping Jade with her two kids as her husband was not at family dinner. It wasn't long till I was left alone with Ma cleaning up after dinner.

"You have any plans tomorrow?" I asked softly.

"Not particularly," Ma hummed, which meant yes, but no more than her usual plans.

"You have time to talk?" I asked, not looking at her.

"For you my dear, yes. You finally gonna tell me who you have been seeing?" she asked slyly. I looked up at her —*how had she known?*

"Jasper, you have been walking around this ranch with your heart glowing out of your chest for weeks. Did you really think I wouldn't notice?" Ma scolded me.

"I just wasn't ready to tell anyone," I grumbled.

"I know, dear. Of course we can chat tomorrow," she patted my shoulder and hugged me before exiting the kitchen, leaving me with all the dirty dishes. *Split the work, my ass.*

I sent Sparrow off to work in a happy post orgasm buzz. I had woken up early and spent twenty minutes this morning worshiping her pussy between her thighs. Teasing orgasm after orgasm from her body grounded me enough to have this conversation with Ma. I hadn't told Sparrow about my plan; I would tell her after work. I needed to do this.

I made my way to the main house to talk to Ma, who was in the kitchen cleaning up after breakfast, which had been a messy affair since Jade's children had slept over. There were small chunks of pancake everywhere.

“Ma,” I greeted, hugging her.

“Morning dear,” she said, smiling at me.

“Is this a coffee or stronger conversation?” she asked, with not an ounce of judgment.

“Spiked coffee,” I offered, nervously. *Fuck, this was hard.* Neither of us talked as Ma busied herself making us each a cup of coffee and splashing a healthy amount of alcoholic coffee creamer in both.

“So this woman you have been seeing?” she asked, taking a sip of her coffee.

“I have been seeing someone,” I admitted. Ma waited for me to share what I wanted to.

“I have been for a while, well on and off, but recently it's gotten serious,” I started, finding it easier to talk about our relationship and keeping Sparrow's name out of it for now.

“How serious?” She asked calmly, but I could see her excitement boiling in her eyes.

“She is basically living with me, and I am considering asking her to move in,” I said before busying myself with my coffee.

“I want to meet the woman who’s got my boy's heart,” Ma cooed, and my gut dropped.

"That's the thing," I grumbled. Ma shot me a look that, when translated, screamed "*WHAT??*" at me.

"Our relationship is. . ." I struggled to find the words to explain what was the issues with our relationship. *Nothing and everything.*

"Complicated?" Ma asked.

"Who I am seeing is. . ." And once again I could not find the words.

"She is younger," I finally admitted, finding that fact easier to admit. Ma just sat there waiting, her eyebrows slowly raising.

"By 12 years," I mumbled.

"So she is what, twenty-one?" Ma asked, frowning.

"Twenty-two," I corrected. Ma let out a sigh.

"You had me worried, boy," Ma snapped at me, a teasing edge to her tone.

"You're fine with that?" I pressed looking at her a little shocked. I wasn't quiet over my issues with our age gap, and she took it in stride without blinking.

"You are both adults," Ma pointed out, shrugging.

"She is also a Swallow Road employee," I admitted finding it easier to keep going now that I was on a roll. As predicted, she took this fact a little worse.

"Jasper," Ma smacked my arm with her hand. She froze then, her mind going through the list of people it could be, which was a short list of one. Her eyes turned to me, the question etched into them.

"You are seeing. . ." Ma started.

"Sparrow," I finished for her. Ma stayed quiet for several moments before drying off her hands and turning to me.

"Can you go feed my chickens? I will be right out," Ma requested, her voice soft and even. She was hiding what she really thought. I nodded, leaving the main house and heading over to where Ma's chickens were. It took me less than five minutes to feed Ma's beloved birds. She joined me just as I was finishing up.

Ma waved her hand, at me requesting it, and I placed my hand in her outstretched one. She placed something small and cold there, folding my hand around it before I could see.

"I had one made for each of you," Ma whispered, holding my closed hand. In my hand sat a ring, one of the rings she had worn on her hand. I knew Jade had gotten one on her wedding day, but I didn't understand why I was getting this one now.

"I had hoped you boys would use them, when you were ready, to welcome *the one* to the family," Ma said, letting go of my hand. In her own words, Ma had admitted that she was giving me the ring she had kept so that I could propose one day. And she was giving it to me after just finding out about me and Sparrow. I opened my hand looking down at the simple band. *She was the one.*

"I would say no rush, but I want my grand-babies," Ma jested, smiling at me. All I wanted to do was go running to Sparrow to babble at her over how much Ma's excitement meant to me. But doing that would mean admitting that I was planning on asking her to marry me. *Not today, but one day.* And interrupting her work day.

After tucking the ring into an inner pocket, I bid Ma goodbye and headed to work myself, feeling lighter and heavier than ever before.

I managed to keep myself from blurting my news at Sparrow all through work, which had gotten easier in the afternoon. I was working with the horses and she wasn't nearby. As I walked towards my truck to head home to the woman I loved. *My sunflower.* I spotted her talking to Caleb by her car.

Before I could stop myself, I drifted over to them.

"You don't know that," Sparrow exclaimed at Caleb.

"Don't know what?" I asked, standing beside Caleb looking at Sparrow.

"Nothing. Just needed romance advice," Caleb muttered darkly.

"Hit me with it," I smiled at him. Caleb looked nervous.

"No offense man but I have never seen *you* with a woman romantically, let alone a relationship. I'm not taking your romance advice, boss," Caleb chuckled at me.

"I'm currently dating—" I tried to explain.

"I gotta get back to Salami," Sparrow announced, cutting me off. She ran away from the conversation, and I dropped the topic. *Had I been wrong to tell Ma without checking with her?*

Minutes later, I walked into my house, the ring still in my pocket weighing a million tons.

"Hey," I greeted a comfy Sparrow. She had changed into pj's and was cuddling with Salami on the couch.

"Hey," she responded sadly.

"What's up, Sunflower?" I asked, crouching down in front of her, my knees protested slightly.

"It's been a month," she whispered into her knees.

"It has," I agreed.

"I want to be loved loudly; I don't want to be a secret," Sparrow admitted, almost sounding angry.

"I couldn't stand there and listen to you lie to Caleb," she whispered as a tear rolled down her cheek.

"Oh, Sunflower," I wiped the tear from her face.

"I was gonna tell him I was dating you," I admitted to her. She looked up at me, a little startled.

"I told Ma this morning, and I am gonna talk to my Pa soon," I promised her.

"You told Mama H?" Sparrow gasped, sitting up on the couch.

"Yeah, I'm serious about this; about us. I love you," I reassured her, before leaning down and kissing her tear damp cheek.

Jasper

I woke up with Sparrow cuddled in my arms and Salami sleeping at our feet. *This was the life. I loved this woman with my whole heart.* Ma's ring still sat in my pocket that was left abandoned on the floor. I kissed Sparrow on her head before sneaking from the bed. I needed somewhere safe to put the ring. We had only been dating officially for a month —a ring now would send her running.

I tugged the ring from my pants pocket and looked through the dark room. It was two in the morning and normally I would have gone back to sleep with Sparrow, but we had fallen asleep quickly, and I was wide awake now.

I finally decided that hiding the ring in my truck was the best course of action as we didn't spend much time there, and Sparrow was never there alone. I had half a mind to attach it to my key ring and have it with me everyday as a promise to myself for the future, but I didn't want to risk it. I flipped open the lid on the center console and tucked the ring safely in there. I sat looking out the windshield at the stars, my hand resting on the gearshift and my fingers tucked into the fabric of Sparrow's panties still wrapped around it.

It wasn't long till I was back inside, wrapping myself around my Sunflower.

"You busy Pa?" I asked, kicking the toe of my boot through the dust.

"Your Ma wants me to build her a new chicken coop," Pa grumbled.

"Want to go for a ride with me?" I asked, stuffing my hands into the back pocket of my jeans. He took me in, my boots making a storm cloud of dust around my feet —a dead give away of my nervousness.

"You got something you need to get off your chest," he grunted —not a question, but a statement.

He didn't wait for me to reply, just walked towards the barn to start tacking up his horse. It wasn't long till the two of us were slowly walking down the path away from the barn. Our horses strolled shoulder to shoulder down the path.

We had both stayed silent as we moved farther and farther from the barn into our land. The morning was cool, the sky bright and cloudless. Ever since Ma had given me the ring and I had hidden it in my truck, it had burned a hole in my mind.

"So you gonna spit it out?" Pas asked, breaking the silence. I grunted at him, not having the words yet. *Why was talking to my Pa different than Ma?*

"It's about a woman, isn't it?" Pa asked, and I nodded, dipping behind the brim of my hat.

"Is she pregnant?" Pa asked, his voice deep but neutral.

"What?" I spluttered.

"Cause if she is, you need to. . ." Pa started to lecture.

"She is not," I interjected.

"Ok," Pa lapsed into silence, waiting for me to continue.

"I'm seeing someone," I admitted quietly to the background sound of our horses hooves in the dusty dirt.

"I'm gonna ask her to move in with me," I followed up.

"That's a big step. How long have you been seeing her?" Pa asked, looking at me from under his own hat.

"Officially? A month, but we had some history before that," I answered. Pa had been a great father, he had taught us all the meaning of family and hard work, he had worked long hours in the day and came home and spent time with us in the evenings. While my one-on-one time with him had been rare with three other siblings, he had tried to give us each alone time with him at least once a month. He carved out several hours for each child, to have his undivided attention. Some of my greatest memories were when I was fifteen and he had spent time with me fixing up my first truck together. But Pa was a rough man of the land. He wasn't always the one with the sweetest words and touchy-feel-y conversations. He loved each of us greatly in his own way.

"Some history, huh," Pa smirked at me. I rolled my eyes at him.

"Yeah, something like that," I grumbled.

"You gonna bring her to family dinner before she moves in? Give us a chance to break her in slowly," Pa joked, but he had a point, we were a lot for someone to deal with all at once —well if Sparrow wasn't already used to them.

"That is the thing," I rubbed my chin, the reins shifting in my hand.

"She's already been to family dinner," I admitted. *Here we go.* Pa's eyebrows shot up at me.

"I'm dating Sparrow," I mumbled under my breath.

"Jasper! She is twenty-two!" Pa snapped at me, shocked. He pulled up on his reins, bringing his horse to a stop. I stopped a couple paces in front of him, my head tipped down hiding from his rage.

"I know," I mumbled, feeling like a child being scolded for breaking dishes.

"Does your Ma know?" he grumbled at me, but some of his shock had worn off.

"Yeah, I told her yesterday," I said, trying not to crumble in on myself.

"What'd she say?" he asked cautiously. He knew that he had over reacted a little and he had dialed it back quickly.

"She had already guessed I was seeing someone. She gave me the ring," I admitted nervously, He would know what that meant.

"And demanded grand-babies," I added laughing under my breath.

"That damn woman is crazy for grandchildren," Pa chuckled with me. The tension between us broke and we continued on in comfortable silence.

"Any advice for asking her to move in with me?" I asked after some time passed. Pa let out a loud laugh that rumbled out over the land.

"You are already doing better than I did," Pa chuckled.

"Your Ma and I started living together when we hated each other's guts," Pa chuckled at the memory. Right, they had started off rough. I always forgot that they had hated each other at one point —which was hard to believe given that they had been in love for so long.

"She's pretty much already moved in —her damn dog made itself comfortable in my home. I just want it official. She just doesn't have the strongest trust in our relationship," I rubbed my neck nervously.

"In the beginning I didn't give her a good reason to trust me," I mumbled. Pa shot me a look trying to untangle my admission.

"If she is basically already living with you, I think she trusts your relationship more than you think," Pa reassured me.

"What do you have against her dog?" Pa asked frowning —ranchers tended to have a soft spot for all animals.

"Its a fucking rat. It pissed on my truck," I grumbled quietly. Pa laughed at me.

"Wait till you meet the thing," I grumbled.

"Bring it to the next family dinner. Which Sparrow now has a standing invitation to. Your Ma will expect her to be there," Pa informed me with a look that said *'your ma will have my ass and yours if she doesn't come'.* We turned back towards the barn, both of us having a long list of work to do today.

"Have fun with the chickens," I smirked at him.

"Little shit," Pa grumbled but still smirked at me.

I texted Sparrow before I started to brush out Jackle.

I was just informed you have a standing invite to family dinner and its my ass on the line if you don't join.

"Jasper!" Jett called through the barn.

"We got a newbie here!" Jett called, running towards me.

"What?" I asked frowning at him.

"Horse trailer for a drop off here," Jett hiked his thumb over his shoulder.

"We aren't expecting anyone," I muttered, following Jett as he jogged back towards the entrance. Two yearlings stood outside a trailer.

They had a dull brown coats and were not looking good.

What the hell? The truck hitched up to the trailer was still running. I ran over to the driver.

"What are these doing here?" I asked the man strongly.

"I'm just the wheels, man. I got an order from my boss. Here is the paperwork," he shrugged, handing over a handful of papers. *This was a load of bullshit.* I jumped back as the driver pulled out of our ranch. *What the fuck?*

"What the fuck?" Jett asked, looking at the scared horses.

"Not a fucking clue," I frowned down at the bogus paperwork. Jett and I spent the rest of the day trying to sort out the new additions and figure out what the hell was going on.

I texted Pa, leaving the unread text from Sparrow alone. I had bigger problems right now I'd talk to her at home. *Home. She was my home.*

Pa! Just got two yearlings dumped on us. You know anything about this?

Pa

What the fuck??

Pa joined me and Jett pouring over the shitty paperwork to figure out how this mess had happened. It was not clear; we couldn't figure it out. The only clear aspect of the paperwork was the fact that they were now legally ours, and their vet records were up-to-date. Which was surprising, given the rough shape they had arrived in.

"I will work with them tomorrow once they calm down a little and get some rest," I muttered as I headed out. I had stayed hours later than I normally would, and had yet to let Sparrow know what was going on. *She was gonna be so mad.*

I walked out of Jake's office where we had been holed up for the last several hours and turned towards the barn. I wanted to check on our rescues before turning in. They were asleep. The rest of the barn was dark and full of the sounds of sleeping horses. I called Sparrow as I made my way to my truck, finally heading home. It was late but she wouldn't be in bed yet —I hoped.

"Where the hell are you?" Sparrow demanded through the phone with no greeting.

"I'm sorry, I know. I am on my way home. It's been a fucking hell of a day," I apologized as I turned my truck on.

"Are you ok?" Sparrow demanded.

"Yes, just really fucking tired and pissed off," I tossed my hat on to the passenger seat and ran my hands through my hair.

"I made dinner," Sparrow said quietly.

"I'm sorry I missed dinner, Sunflower," I felt bad for missing the dinner that she had taken the time to make for me.

"You are almost home, right? I will reheat it for you," she said, the sounds of her moving around the kitchen floating through the phone.

"Just down the road," I hummed. We stayed on the line till I was right at my door. I stepped through the door and Salami came wiggling over to me, excited to see me home. The whole house smelled amazing.

"Hello, Sunflower," I whispered into her hair as I pulled her close to me. She melted into my body, her head nuzzling into my chest.

"Hello," she mumbled softly. She sounded sleepy.

"I'm sorry I am late," I apologized.

"I don't care that you are late. I get it. I care that you didn't let me know," Sparrow grumbled in my arms.

"We are both gonna have long days and late days, but we need to keep each other in the loop. I would have started dinner later if I had known," Sparrow complained.

"I love you," I promised.

"I love you too," Sparrow replied, smiling. My heart thundered in my chest at those three —well four— words. *She was mine.*

"Dinner?' Sparrow asked, pulling out of my arms.

"I'd love some. What did you make?" I asked, walking over to the kitchen. I still had my muddy boots on, and hat on my head. Sparrow smirked at me, before reaching up and grabbing my hat from me.

"Sparrow," I warned her. With a devilish grin, Sparrow dropped my hat on to her head.

"Sparrow. Wear the hat…" I smirk at her.

"Ride the cowboy," Sparrow finished pulling on my shirt, her lips landing on mine. *Fuck, she tastes so good.* My hand slid down her back, my fingers digging into her ass. Sparrow let out a small moan into my mouth. Her body pressed into me, her hips pressing into mine.

"Sparrow," I mumble into her mouth.

"More kiss, less talk," Sparrow groaned into my mouth.

"The food," I pointed out, pulling away from her.

"Fuck," Sparrow cursed, running to the stove where the dish she was heating up was bubbling all over my stove. *Oh well.*

I watched her poke at the pot, trying to save the dinner she had made me, her back to me.

"Live with me," I blurted out to her back. Sparrow hummed at me, not fully paying attention to what I said.

"Sorry, what was that?" Sparrow asked, looking over her shoulder.

"Live with me," I repeated nervously rubbing my hands over my dirty jeans. Sparrow looked at me for several beats before opening her mouth.

"Not when you walk around our house in your boots," Sparrow commented as she turned back to the food. *Was that a yes?* I kicked my boots off and shoved them beside hers at the door. I padded over to her, sliding my arms around her waist, resting my head on her shoulder.

"Better?" I asked, kissing her shoulder.

"Much," Sparrow laughed, handing me a bowl of cheesy tomato pasta.

"Thank you, Sunflower." I kissed her cheek, taking the bowl. I slumped down into a chair at my dining room table. *I could get used to this.*

"So?" I questioned as she sat down next to me. A bowl of chocolate ice cream before her. Sparrow raised her eyebrows at me.

"Will you live with me?" I asked before shoving a large mouthful of pasta in my mouth.

"Well, now that you have actually asked," Sparrow sassed at me rolling her eyes.

"Sparrow," I warned.

"I don't know," Sparrow mused, digging around in her ice cream bowl with her spoon.

"Sunflower, you basically already live here," I said after swallowing my mouthful.

"But all my stuff is there," Sparrow pointed out.

"I can store it here, and we can convert the spare bedroom into a space for you so you can have your own space here," I offered, watching emotions dance through her eyes. Sparrow looked unsure.

"It's a lot," Sparrow whispered.

"You aren't ready to move in," I tried to hide the rejection from my tone.

"It's just so fast," Sparrow fidgeted under my gaze —goddamn she looks young right now. *Fuck. I forget she's only twenty-two.*

"I'm serious about us," I mumbled quietly.

"You weren't a month ago!" Sparrow pointed out loudly.

"I was scared," I raised my voice at her slightly —not in anger but in panic.

"I still am, but this, us, is it for me," I explained pointing between us. Sparrow's face drained. *Oh fuck, I went too far.*

Fuck, I just admitted that this was end game for me. One month into dating. I was so fucking screwed.

"You are serious?" Sparrow echoed.

"Yes," I admitted.

"You want me to live here," Sparrow said, pointing her finger into the table.

"Yes, Sparrow," I rolled my eyes at her. Sparrow snorted and then started to laugh at the top of her lungs.

"Roll your eyes at me one more time," Sparrow warned playfully. I pushed my chair back from the table, patting my hand on my thigh.

"What you gonna do about it?" I asked, leveling my eyes at her smirking. Sparrow got up and darted around the table, sliding in between my legs and sat down in my lap.

"I will make your eyes roll for a whole different reason," Sparrow whispered in my ear. My dick that was already hard in my pants jerked against my jeans.

"You better follow through with that, Sunflower," I groaned as I nipped at her shoulder.

"Please just think about living with me," I begged into her shoulder.

"You sound so good begging," Sparrow purred. *Fuck, the mouth on this woman.*

"Do you want me on my knees, Sunflower?" I purred back at her. Sparrow blushed at my words, but nodded, smiling at me.

I lifted her ass from my lap and slowly sank to my knees in front of her.

"Sparrow," I started.

"Please will you shower with me?" I begged letting my voice drop to a smoky tone. Sparrow let out a small moan as she stood there looking down at me on my knees for her.

"I'd love to," she whispered, holding out her hand to pull me up off the floor.

"Any time you want me on my knees, you just have to ask, Sunflower," I said, chuckling as I pulled her down to the floor with me.

"A shower would be great," I whispered into her lips before kissing her with all the meaning behind how serious I was about her.

SPARROW

Jasper had picked me up and thrown me over his shoulder —which I thought only happened in romance movies. He set me down on the sink counter. Jasper tugged off his shirt, revealing his tanned, powerful body underneath. I drank him in, his low slung jeans hugging his hips.

"Enjoying the view?" Jasper asked as he bent over to start the shower.

"Very much," I gigged, starting to pull off my shirt. Jasper undid his belt, his jeans sitting loose and open on his hips. *Fuck.*

"Sunflower, stop eye fucking me and get in the shower," Jasper chuckled as he pushed his jeans off his delicious thighs. *Was I drooling?* Jasper stepped into the steaming shower, and I scrambled to get the rest of my clothes off and join him.

I jumped under the rainfall shower head; it was large enough for both of us to stand under the water. Jasper smirked, his eyes running down my body and watching the water fall down me. Jasper reached up, his large palm landed on my throat gently pulling me towards him, my breasts brushing his chest as he turned around to press me against the tiled wall.

I gasped at the cold tile on my back, his large hand resting against me. Jasper's greedy lips met mine, and the pressure on my neck increased as Jasper's body leaned into mine. We devoured each other, hands desperately grabbing at one another's bodies. The hot water cascaded down our bodies, keeping us warm. *Fuck the water bill, apparently.*

"Sunflower," Jasper groaned against my skin.

Jasper thrust his dick against my thigh, seeking some relief. He rutted into my thighs, the head of his cock gliding past my clit with each thrust. My tongue was still tangled in his mouth as I reached down with my hand, wrapping it around his solid dick.

He was hot in my hand, his skin soft under my touch. *Fuck he feels so good. Was he this big every time?* I tightened my grip on his dick slightly, Jasper's groan music to my ears. Jasper thrust into the palm of my hand.

"How's my good boy?" I purred as he sought his pleasure.

"Horny as fuck," Jasper growled against my lips.

"Me too," I smirked at him. I let go of his dick. It dropped slightly under its own weight before bobbing back up.

Jasper's fingers brushed over my peaked nipple, the rough pad of his fingers feeling amazing under the hot water.

"Would you like some relief from your horniness?" I asked, batting my eyes at him suggestively.

"What do you have in mind?" Jasper whispered, nipping at my ear.

I sank to my knees, the water falling on my back, I wrapped my hand around the base of his cock. I looked up at him, my eyes tracking over his strong thighs, powerful hips, and muscled chest. Jasper looked down at me, watching as his cock disappeared into my mouth. I licked at his cock, his head in my mouth. I tipped my head back, gently pulling his cock deeper into my mouth. Jasper groaned, his hand resting on the top of my head.

Slowly, I sucked on him, hollowing out my cheeks. Then, as I released the pressure, I pulled back, letting the head of his cock rub against the roof of my mouth. I repeated this over and over, keeping up a good rhythm. Jasper's hands dug into my scalp, pulling at my hair, our moans echoing around the shower with us.

I gently let my teeth scrape over his skin, the musky flavour of his pre-cum sliding over my tongue and down my throat. Jasper's hands guided my head to a faster pace, the gentle pressure of his hands on the back of my head.

"Such a good girl," Jasper praised. Jasper thrust his hips into my mouth, fucking my face.

Jasper pulled my head back, letting the head of his cock rest on my lips. I licked the fresh bead of pre-cum that welled up before me. Jasper leaned down to kiss me, his lips licking over my mouth and tasting his pre-cum on my lips.

"Dirty girl," Jasper whispered.

"I'm gonna make you scream my name," Jasper purred as he gently rubbed his hands over my pussy, spreading the unscented soap over my skin. Jasper and I finished washing up ourselves, throwing dirty flirty comments at each other.

I stepped out of the shower, pulling my towel from the towel warmer sitting by the sink. I wrapped the plush toasty towel around my body. Jasper climbed out of the shower behind me, grabbing his own warm towel. Before my towel cooled down, I dried myself off, enjoying the warmth. Jasper dropped his towel onto the sink counter, his fingers tugging at my towel.

"Bend over," Jasper commanded, smirking at me. I dropped my towel to the floor —it pooled around our feet— and bent over the counter. I rested my weight on the towel covered counter, pulling my hips up and onto the counter.

"Fuck," Jasper groaned, his fingers grazing over the curve of my ass that was now promptly on display for him. I shifted my weight slightly, wiggling my ass at him. Jasper's hand pulled back before connecting with my ass again. The soft slap went straight to my core.

"Look at me," Jasper gritted looking at me through the mirror. I looked up and met his eyes. Jasper guided his dick to my ass, letting his dick fall down onto my ass. He felt so warm against my skin.

Jasper pressed his dick against my pussy. *Fuck he is big.* Slowly, my body adjusted to him and he slipped in easily. My arousal coated his dick as he pulled back out of me. He worked his dick into me, taking the time to make sure not to injure me. The angle the counter had me at made things difficult, but it was so hot. I watched him in the mirror as he slowly fucked me. The overwhelming feeling of his dick fully filling me before sliding back out.

Jasper kept thrusting into me slowly, but never coming to a stop. It was infuriating. I wanted him to either pick up his pace and fuck me into the mirror, or to sit fully seated in me and stay there.

"Jasper!" I whined, my hands white knuckling the counter.

"Something wrong, Sunflower?" Jasper asked, smirking down at the sight of his dick parting my pussy and filling me up.

"More," I gritted, as I pushed back into him.

"More did you say?" Jasper chuckled, he stopped fully seated in me, the round curve of my ass against his hips.

"Yes," I begged.

"Naughty sunflower," Jasper purred, his hands dropping to the counter either side of my hips. Jasper thrust into my harder, slowly picking up his pace as he went. The bathroom filled with my breathy moans and the sound of Jasper's hips hitting my ass.

"Shh," Jasper shushed, his hand coming up my body and wrapping around my mouth. I bit my tongue, swallowing down my moans.

"Do you hear that?" Jasper asked as he thrust into me. Under the sound of our bodies colliding I could hear the sweet wet sound of my pussy as Jasper dicked me down.

"You sound so good," Jasper groaned, as he let my mouth go.

We both got lost in the pleasure we were making. The way our bodies worked together to bring us both pleasure.

"Fuck, Sunflower I am close," Jasper's deep voice moaned behind me.

"Fill me up, Jasper," I moaned as his movements faltered, becoming jerky.

"Fuck, Sparrow," Jasper moaned my name as he thrust into my sharply. His dick jerked, thickening even more, as his warm seed filled my pussy. *Fuck, he felt so good.* I orgasmed as Jasper finished in me, my vaginal walls milking every last drop of cum from him.

"Such a good girl, Sunflower," Jasper praised, his dick still sitting in my pussy, keeping his seed in me. A small amount of his cum coated my pussy, and dripped down my thighs, he had filled me past full. Jasper pulled out of me, his still semi hard dick dripping with our combined climax. Grabbing my towel off of the floor, from around our feet, Jasper cleaned me up. I slipped off the counter, my knees wobbly, and took the towel from him. I cleaned off his dick carefully, taking my time.

"Thank you, Sunflower," Jasper kissed me in thanks. I squealed as Jasper leaned down and picked me up, carrying me bridle style to the bed. Jasper held me close under the covers, his thumb drawing circles on my hip. Jasper was deep in thought, his head resting against mine and his lips pressed to my hair.

"Your ass looked so good bent over the counter," Jasper said, breaking the warm silence.

"My ass always looks good," I countered, smiling.

"True, but it looked extra good bent over the counter," Jasper added. He lapsed back into silence, his thumb resuming circles on my hip.

"Have you ever tried anal?" Jasper asked quietly. I paused looking up at him.

"I haven't," I answered, carefully.

"Would you consider trying it with me?" Jasper asked slowly, as carefully chose his words.

"Have you tried it?" I asked, avoiding answering his question. *I needed a moment to think.*

"No. I haven't really felt the desire to... till now," Jasper admitted.

"We can try it," I finally answered. I wasn't sure if his lack of experience was a positive or negative, but being of equal inexperience in at least this part of life felt good. While our age gap didn't bother me nine days out of the week, it felt good to not be the only one this was new for.

"You sure?" Jasper asked.

"We can try it, if we both like it we can discuss if it's something we do regularly," I reassured. Jasper nodded against my hair.

"Naughty boy wants to fuck my ass," I giggled.

"Naughty girl wants her ass fucked," Jasper countered. We self-destructed into a laugh attack.

Jasper brushed away the tears of laughter from his face and leaned down to kiss me softly —slow and gentle like my romance novels.

"Watching my dick fuck your pussy with your ass in the air was so hot, and I couldn't stop thinking about fucking your ass," Jasper whispered against my lips, punctuating each word with a kiss. I pulled away, settling back into his arms. I could feel Jasper's hard cock press into my back.

I pressed my ass into his boner, subtly grinding into him.

"Sunflower," Jasper warned, his voice low.

"Want to try it now?" I asked under my breath.

"One round not enough to sate you, Sunflower?" Jasper asked, his voice deep and gravely.

"Never," I purred biting my lip.

"Does my naughty girl need her ass fucked?" Jasper asked, his fingers dipping between my thighs to my throbbing pussy.

"Yes," I breathed, leaning back into him and spreading my legs as his finger started to work my clit. "Good girl," Jasper purred into my ear.

Sparrow

Jasper had told his parents about us, and while he had not out right told anyone else, he was less guarded about his affection with me.

"You are still at work, Sunflower. It's called professionalism," Jasper scolded jokingly after I had slapped his ass. I bit my lip trying not to laugh at his fake serious face.

"Go back to work, woman," Jasper teased, smiling at me, and as I turned from him to go back to work, his hand darted out and smacked me on the ass. I looked up to see Caleb standing there, his face painted with plain shock. I tipped my head back and started laughing. I skipped over and wrapped my arm around Caleb's shoulders, walking with him away from Jasper.

"That is who you are seeing?" Caleb hissed at me under his breath.

I glanced over my shoulder to look at Jasper, who was looking a little spooked, his head tipped down to hide his blush under the brim of his hat. *Oh poor baby.*

"Yeah," I giggled at Caleb.

"Can you get me a raise?" Caleb asked jokingly.

"Get in line," I pushed on Caleb's shoulders gently.

Caleb and I spent the day baking under the sun. We were in a far field digging out an old irrigation system. We sat under the shade of the tractor we had been using as we ate lunch. Caleb kept looking over at me as if he was gonna ask something, and then looked away changing his mind.

"What do you want to know?" I asked, rolling my eyes at him.

"How-good-is-he-in-bed? How-much-older-is-he? Has-he-told-anyone-yet? How-serious-is-it? How-big-is-his-dick?" Caleb rushed out question after question, stumbling over his words. I waited a moment to see if he was done.

Caleb was blushing, and it had nothing to do with the sun.

"Caleb, that's a lot of questions about his dick, is there something I should know?" I asked, wiggling my brows at him.

"Shut up," Caleb dismissed me, playfully.

"Umm. Amazing. Older. Yes. Very," I answered each of his questions with a one word answer. Caleb chewed on his food as he digested the new information.

"He asked me to move in with him," I confessed. The speed that Caleb's head snapped around to me needed to be studied for world records.

"He is fucking cooked for you," Caleb snickered.

"Don't you mean whipped?" I rolled my eyes at him as he continued to wheeze beside me.

"But you should move in with him," Caleb finally managed to get out once he regained his ability to breathe again.

"He is loving you loudly," Caleb reasoned.

"I do basically already live there," I conceded. Slipping my phone out my back pocket, to text Jasper.

Better get some boxes. You have some packing to do ;) I plan on sitting back and watching your ass while I drink.

Jasper

My ass does look great in these jeans. :P

As our work day came to a close, Caleb whistled and lifted something from his lunch bag. A bottle of Crown Whiskey.

"Just wait until everyone finds out you're screwing the boss," Caleb said, handing me the bottle. We took turns tipping back the bottle of Blackberry Crown. It didn't take long under the sun, after a long day of work for us both to be tipsy. Caleb started to blast tunes from his phone sitting on the tractor as we cleaned up for the day.

"I'm driving back," I gurgled waving my hand at him.

"No, you are drunk. I will drive this big piece of machinery back," Caleb said, swinging his arms at the tractor.

"You are drunk too," I pointed out.

"You both are," a deep voice said from behind us. It was Jasper.

"Jasper!" I squealed, running towards him. He didn't bulk at my mud covered overalls, and welcomed me into his arms.

"Sunflower," he greeted, picking me up and spinning me around.

"I came to see how it all turned out," Jasper said as he placed my feet back in the dirt. He stood there, his feet parted slightly in the dirt, his hands resting on his hips.

"It turned out great," I said, swinging around a little too fast.

I almost fell over as I came to a stop, pointing out over the ground we had worked.

"Ok, Sunflower. Looks great," Jasper said from behind me, his hands grabbing my waist.

"It's ok, Caleb knows," I whisper-hissed to Jasper as he pulled me around to him by my overall straps.

"Does he now?" Jasper whispered, leaning down to kiss me, his hat shielding my view. I hummed contently as Jasper slowly pulled back.

"I'll drive the tractor back, you two should climb in," Jasper said, taking the bottle of whiskey from Caleb and slinging back his own mouthful of liquor. Caleb and I scrambled to hold on to the tractor as Jasper pulled out of the field and towards home. Jasper talked Caleb into restarting the music. By the time we were half way home Caleb and I were hanging off the cab. I was half ass dancing while trying not to fall off the moving tractor. Caleb and Jasper were singing at the top of their lungs. It had not taken Jasper long to catch up with our buzz.

Jasper parked the tractor in its home, and I jumped down from the perch I had clung to. Caleb kept the music playing as several of the other ranch hands came over, drawn by the laughter and music.

It wasn't long until we were all unwinding around the tractor, beers were cracked, and laughter flowed. I sat on the engine cover, my legs swinging to the beat of the music and watched Jasper relaxed and chatting with the other farm hands. Until I was dared to start stripping on the tractor.

"She strips, you strip," Jasper snapped, frowning. While that got some whistles and my darer was pressured into also stripping, they ended up backing down.

"Boxes are in my truck," Jasper whispered to me, winking over his can of beer. The impromptu party fell apart as everyone got hungry. Long days and hard work and all that, made us a hungry bunch, and honestly most of us needed something to absorb some of the alcohol we consumed.

Jasper drove my tipsy butt to my apartment to a very excited and grumpy Salami.

"I'm sorry, my baby boy," I cooed at him on my knees with my arms spread out to him. He wiggled over to me, but then peeled off and ran away as he got close to me. He was holding a grudge over my late return to him. Jasper got his regular greeting.

"Sit your ass down," Jasper commanded, pointing to my half made bed. *Yes, sir.* I settled down on the mattress and watched as Jasper set down the empty collapsed boxes in the middle of my small apartment. Jasper pulled a colourful can from his back pocket; it was wrapped in a bright orange sticky note.

He held out the can to me and smiled. The sticky note had Jasper's large print on it. *Hot Brat Juice.* I peeled back the note and found my favorite premixed cocktail in a can. Spiked grapefruit-aid made with vodka from a local distillery.

"Enjoy, Sunflower," Jasper leaned down and kissed me, tasting of beer and whiskey.

"Snackies," I giggled, holding out my hands and opening and closing them like a toddler. Jasper chuckled, leaving the half filled box he was working on and coming over to me. Which earned him having my stick paws grabbing at him. I was happily more drunk than tipsy.

"Want to go out for dinner?" Jasper asked, pulling me from my place on the bed.

"I'm a little drunk," I said, leaning on him.

"We can get take out," Jasper offered. That was how twenty minutes later, I was waiting in Jasper's truck as he ran inside the little local pizza place *Lonnie's Pizza and Wings* had the best cheese bread and perfect greasy pizza.

"Hold this for me, Sunflower," Jasper asked, handing me the three box stack of cardboard boxes.

"And for you," he said, handing me a mango and raspberry milkshake.

"Thank you," I hummed, before sipping on the cold beverage. If I was a cartoon, I would have hearts jumping from my eyes.

"I know moving in is a big step, so soon," Jasper said, as he pulled back onto the road. We had danced around the topic of my moving in with him the whole time I had watched him pack.

"I think I was more spooked with the idea of permanently living with you, more than the reality," I spoke around the straw of my drink.

"I can't wait for our life together," Jasper whispered as he looked out the windshield at the sun setting in front of us. *He sounded like he meant more than me living with him.*

We sat in the middle of my apartment, on the floor, laughing as we ate too much pizza and cheese bread.

"I love you, Sunflower," Jasper nuzzled into my shoulder. Our buzz had worn off half way through the pizza.

I had been living with Jasper officially for a week. It was the best week of my life. It had taken me some time to unpack or store the rest of my things. Jasper had kept his word about converting the spare room into a space for me. I just didn't know what to do with it. For now, it housed my boxes of books.

Jasper was working with one of the new horses today, and I was done early. So of course I ran home, got changed out of my mud soaked jeans, and into a pair of my favorite overalls. A couple months ago I had gotten my best friend Mia to embroider small blue flowers along the cuffs and straps of them.

I picked up some snacks from Jasper's kitchen—*ours*— it's our kitchen now. That was gonna take some time. I was home for all of ten minutes —eight of which I snuggled with Salami who had adapted to living full time with Jasper within minutes of the move. I ran out the door with a happy Salami in tow.

Salami and I sat up post on the fence of the paddock turned training area. Jasper stood in the middle as the horse danced around him. He waited, giving the horse more space to test him. Jasper did not fold, each time the horse tried to get past him and get the upper hand, Jasper moved, stepping in the horses way, sending it skittering off away from him; watching him in his element was pantie dropping, watching him hold on to his power over a five hundred pound beast was pantie melting.

I sat there drinking in the warmth of the sun, watching my man, and enjoying my snacks. Salami ran around the paddock for several minutes before setting down in a patch of sunlight and watching Jasper from under the fence. Jasper had seen me on the fence and smiled at me, tipping his hat in greeting. I was tempted to flash him, but didn't want to risk unplanned eyes.

Jasper slowly eased towards the horse till he was touching the flank of the animal. It just stood there, mild signs of stress, but no red flags. Jasper took a hold of the rope tied to the western bridle it was wearing and started to walk the new horse back towards the barn. I hopped down from the fence, packing up my snack wrappers.

My head was turned away, the sun shining in my eyes, but my skin bristled with warning. I looked over as Jasper tried to guide the horse through the gate, my heart slamming into my chest as I stood there frozen as I watched the horse rear up before bolting, dragging Jasper across the ground with him, his hand caught up in the reins.

Jasper was dragged for several feet before he managed to let go of the reins, his body slamming hard into the ground. He didn't move. *He didn't move!* My mind spun in place, then like a switch, my brain went from freeze to fight. I bolted towards the fence, vaulting over the wooden beams and into the paddock.

I ran towards Jasper, the horse spooking slightly as I ran. He was laying on his side, folded, his chest rising and falling but out cold. Fuck. Fuck. *Fuck!*

"Jasper!" I begged, kneeling in the dirt next to him. My hands hovered over his body; I was scared to touch him. I had no clue if he had any broken bones, if he had injured his spine, or hit his head.

Tears spilled down my face as I knelt before the man I loved. The deep thud of hooves echoed up through my knees, and I looked up to see the horse looping round, headed right for me. I scrambled to my feet, locking eyes with the horse. It looked so scared, its eyes bugging out of its head. Standing a couple feet in front of Jasper, I planted my feet, trying to muster up enough courage to give off a strong enough vibe that it decided against testing me.

Much like Jasper had earlier, the horse kept dancing closer and then backed away when I didn't back down. After we went through this dance several times, the buzzing and spinning in my head slowed down. *Nothing like standing in the way of a scared five hundred pound animal.*

I pulled my phone from my back pocket, hitting the letter H into my contact search bar and hitting the first one that came up. My phone was in my hand and my eyes on the horse as it danced away from me again.

"This is Jake. Leave a message at the tone." I hung up, not leaving a message. I hit the next H in the list. *Please.*

"Jasper. I will get back to you when I'm not busy."

Fuck! The next person. The phone rang in my hand, I was starting to get desperate.

"Sparrow? What's up my dear?" the gentle voice of Mama H asked as she picked up. *Oh, thank fuck!*

"Mama H! Come quick! It's Jasper. He got knocked down and he hasn't gotten up," I garble into the phone in a panic.

"We are coming," Mama H said, her voice strong and calm. It felt like a lifetime before I heard the sound of the four wheeler.

And then Mama H was there atop the four wheeler, she came riding round the corner like a soldier atop a dragon. My heart broke in my chest with relief seeing her determined face. It was a full five minutes before Jett and Papa H came round the corner after Mama H. Mama H was still in her apron, the signs of her dinner plans all over it. She was wearing two different shoes, and only one foot had a sock on it.

Mama H had come running, nothing stopping the mama bear from getting to her cub —full grown cub as it was. Mama H spotted me standing in the middle of the paddock, mere feet from a horse. Jett jumped over the fence and headed straight for the horse. Papa H opened the gate, and Mama H ran straight for me.

"We are here honey," Mama H cooed, wrapping her arms around me. "Jasper," I choked into her shoulder.

With Jett having handled the horse, he guided the upset animal out of the way. Papa H and Jett set to work jerry—rigging a trailer into a stretcher to safely carry Jasper back home. The shock caught up with me and I crumbled in Mama H's arms as she held me, barking orders at the two men to get '*my baby back home safe*'.

Jasper's eyes opened with a loud groan right before Jett was about to pull out.

"Hey man," Jett said, coming to stand by his younger brother. I couldn't hear what Jasper said to Jett, his words getting lost in the wind.

"Sunflower?" Jett asked, frowning at his brother. *Sunflower.* I can't lose him. "Blue," Jasper choked out before he lost consciousness again. The rest of the evening was a blur.

We were back at the main house in a flash. At some point, someone had called an ambulance which now waited by the main house. Then I was back home —the home I had just started sharing with Jasper. Then I was in Jade's car as she drove us to the hospital. I had spent hours sitting in the stiff plastic chairs in the hospital waiting room, the whole Harlow clan around me.

"Two of my boys in the hospital in one year," Mama H muttered, shaking her head.

"I'm looking for Mrs. Harlow?" a man in scrubs asked, walking up to our group.

"That's me," Mama H said, standing up.

"Jasper is awake, which is great news. He's in a good amount of pain so we have him on some painkillers. He doesn't have any long term injuries which is a miracle. He has a concussion, and mild spinal shock," the nurse explained the treatment options. Jasper would be home by the end of the week, and barring any complications he would be back at work soon after that.

He was ok.

JASPER

Four months later

Sparrow hadn't found the ring yet, though there had been a couple close calls. While we had kept our relationship on the down low from the other employees, there had been a couple rumors around us which had died down a month ago. My accident had scared her, and hearing about how she had jumped into the ring to protect me from the spooked horse had felt like something out of a movie. The first two weeks after I got home, she had hovered over me, but as my pain receded and I returned to work, the overprotective side melted away and we settled into our old routine again.

She hadn't shown any further sign of being over her fear of horses —maybe it was just that her love for me had been stronger. Sparrow came barreling into the house, her arms filled with shopping bags.

"Hello, Sunflower," I greeted, giving her a quick kiss.

"Hello," she said back to me as she set her bags on the counter.

Sparrow started to unpack, groceries filling all the counter space.

"I got you a gift," Sparrow said, holding out a handful of fabric. It was a plain black silk dress shirt.

"Thank you, Sunflower," I said holding it up to my chest.

"I thought you'd look good in it," she hummed as she continued to put away the groceries.

The last bag was filled with replacement work clothes for the both of us, and a large number of different bottles I didn't recognize.

"What's all this?" I asked picking up a bottle.

"For my hair," Sparrow waved her hand over her head indicating the slightly faded blue with her natural color peaking through.

"Can I help?" I asked placing the bottle back down. Sparrow looked slightly startled at me asking to participate in doing her hair.

"Yeah, that would be amazing," she replied, smiling softly.

"When do you want to do it?" I asked, walking over to her as she put the last of the food away.

"Tonight?" she suggested with a slight shrug.

"Perfect," I leaned down and pressed a soft kiss to her lips before scooping her up in my arms and carrying her up the stairs.

Dying Sparrow's hair took way longer than I had expected. She sat at the end of our bed, wringing her wet hair out. We had done her roots with the blue, and touched up the rest of the blue hair. Then added on another layer of the black dye on her ends. Sparrow was dressed in an old work shirt of mine that had been headed for the garbage, but I wasn't so sure now. It looked so good on her, the softness of watching her sit there with a towel in hand and her hair wet.

I had spent the last two months trying to plan how I was gonna ask her to marry me, but nothing seemed to fit. Nothing had felt like us; nothing had felt right to capture our love. I was just as surprised as she was when the words tumbled out of my mouth. I had settled behind her, and she had leaned back, resting her head against me. I had been thinking about how perfect this felt, and then the words just fell out of my mouth. At first, I wasn't sure if I had said them or just thought about it.

"Marry me."

"What?" Sparrow asked after a moment. *What had I just said?*

"Marry me," I repeated.

"Do you mean like at some point in the future maybe or…" Sparrow let the unsaid words hang in the air. She had crawled from my lap and knelt on the bed next to me.

"Sparrow. Will you marry me?" I asked, reaching out to cradle her face in my palm. She melted into my touch for a moment.

"Jasper," she sighed. I closed my eyes, waiting for the rejection. It was too soon.

"Don't just ask me cause. . .cause," Sparrow stumbled through her words and ended up with her flapping her hand through the air to indicate the words she meant to say.

"Cause what?" I asked, inching closer to her.

"Cause you think its the next step," Sparrow finished dully.

"Sunflower. I want you to be my wife," I whispered, tucking some of her wet hair behind her ear.

"We should…you should think about it a little more. You know, just to make sure this is really what you want," Sparrow argued. She was protesting a lot, but I had yet to hear her say no.

"Sparrow. Your ring has been burning a hole in my mind for months. If you give me two seconds, I can go grab it," I reassured her.

"My ring?" she asked. I could hear the hidden excitement in her voice. I nodded, pulling myself from our bed.

"Two seconds," I promised before bolting from the room and running to my truck. Sparrow was still sitting on the bed, in my shirt, just like when I had left her there. I flung my body on to the bed beside her and crawled my way over to her.

"Will you marry me?" I asked again, holding out the ring to her.

"On one condition," Sparrow giggled. I nodded, waiting to hear what ass backwards request she had.

"You ask me again, on your knees," Sparrow whispered in my ear.

"You know you only have to ask and I will always get down on my knees for you," I whispered before sliding from the bed and sinking to my knees. Sparrow glowed as she smiled down at me, her hands floating over her chin.

"Yes," she whispered, her hands fluttering slightly before she wrapped her arms and legs around me. I picked her up, spinning her around the room before falling back onto the bed with her in my arms.

I gently slipped the simple silver band onto her finger. It rested beautifully on top of the ring she already wore. She held up her hand, looking at the new ring on her finger. She didn't complain or comment about the simple silver band. She didn't care there was no large rock on her ring.

Sparrow pulled the ring off of her finger. Before I could protest, she pulled her other ring off and slipped mine back on. Holding up her hand again to look at it.

"That's better," she said, smiling and wiggling her fingers at me. I grasped her hand, pulling her knuckles to my lips and kissing my ring on her finger.

Sparrow

Mama H

Family dinner tonight!

Jasper

Got it!

I smiled at my phone. I loved Harlow family dinner. And now that we had come clean about our relationship, I had been effortlessly folded into the mix. I tucked my phone into my back pocket, my rings snagging on the fabric. *My rings. Jasper's ring. Our engagement.* We hadn't told anyone yet —no one had even noticed the new ring on my hand. Which was fine, as I normally wore all plain silver rings on my fingers, but still. I shot Jasper a text in our message thread.

We telling them?

It was all hands on deck, restocking our feed supply. We had ordered a little late, and this truck was much bigger as we were lower on our back stock than normal.

Jasper

We are gonna have to Ma will know the ring.

Jasper had told me about how Mama H had given him the ring, and had told me about the story behind the rings. How Mama H had gotten them made —one for each of her children— and worn them everyday till they were each ready to settle down. Jade had gotten hers as a wedding gift, and Jasper had gotten his when he told her about us. I'm not sure what the difference between the timing was for, but I didn't press it. Family dinner was gonna get interesting.

"Stop texting your *boyfriend* Sparrow and get back to work," Eric joked before letting out a low whistle.

"Yeah, Sparrow," Caleb joined in smirking at me.

"Shut up," I grumbled getting back to work with them. It wasn't much longer before we had everything put away and were done for the day.

As I walked to my car, ready to head home and see Jasper before dinner, I pulled out my phone and saw a text from Jasper from an hour ago.

Jasper

Shower with me after work ;)

On my way home!

In less than five minutes, I was back home. I was greeted by a wiggling Salami, who I let out to go pee. Jasper wasn't home yet. I sat on the steps up to the house texting him while Salami ran around my car.

We need to consider not keeping our relationship secret from the others.

Jasper

Talk about it at home? I will be home in half an hour.

Sure thing.

I whistled for Salami before heading inside, Salami on my heels as I entered the house. I sat in my room on the floor, scrolling through SipFlip for any local second hand furniture in my budget. There was a cute chair I wanted. I messaged the seller and looked around the room. I had thought a walk in closet would be a good idea, but the idea of a cute book nook sounded good too. I looked around the small room. There was a double bed in the room and a generic side table. The closet was small and empty.

There is enough room to do both… I pulled out a sharpie and pulled one of the boxes of books closer, drawing out my half finished idea. One wall being a floor to ceiling bookshelf and the other a built in closet spanning the whole wall. It would take a little bit of DIY renovation but give me a couple weeks, some good tunes and a sledge hammer and I could do it myself.

"Hello, Sunflower," Jasper greeted leaning against the door.

"Hello," I replied, getting up and wrapping him in my arms.

"Shower?" Jasper rumbled into my hair.

"Can't wait," I yelped as he picked me up, wrapping my legs around his waist walking me towards the shower.

"My ring looks so good on you," Jasper purred, bringing my hand to his mouth.

"Thank you," I hummed.

"Know what you want to do with your room?" Jasper asked, looking round the room.

"Still thinking," I mumbled.

"No rush," Jasper responded.

"We should tell the other ranch hands that we are together," I said as I started to undress when Jasper started the shower.

"Isn't that gonna cause problems for you?" Jasper asked as he eye fucked me from across the room.

"We are going to get married," I pointed out.

"We can tell some people," Jasper said, leaning down and giving my lips a quick peck. It took us another half an hour to get out of the shower, and we were running late for family dinner. Jasper drove to the main house and his eyes kept jumping to me as he grinned the whole way there.

"I feel naked," I grumbled as we walked up the stairs. I wiggled my hands in Jasper's face, highlighting my feeling of nakedness. I had left all of my rings off, except for Jasper's ring.

"Ready?" Jasper asked, adjusting the baseball hat on his head nervously.

"Ready," I confirmed. I opened the front door and stepped in. Jake fumbled around the kitchen; his physical therapy was going well.

"Hey everyone!" Jasper called out to the room. I bit my lip waiting for everyone's attention on us.

"I just wanted to introduce the future Mrs. Jasper Harlow," Jasper announced, lift our intertwined fingers. Mama H let out a squeal and launched herself excitedly at her husband. Everyone let out a loud cheer led by Jake, who hugged his brother. Jade came running over to me, baby in her arms, wrapping me in a big hug.

"Finally, some more girls," Jade whisper-squealed in my ear.

"Congratulations," Jett hollered as Mama H grabbed my hand, looking at the silver ring on my hand and tears welling in her eyes. I looked down at her soft wrinkled hands, two plain silver rings sat on her pointer and middle finger. Two more slots for future family members.

Papa Harlow set out a shot glass of whiskey for each person there —minus Jett and the babies.

"To the future Mrs. Jasper Harlow," Papa H toasted before tipping back his shot back. We all followed suit, Jett letting out a loud whoop.

"Get ready for the good old family welcome of putting more work on your plate," Jade toasted laughing.

SPARROW

I sat on the couch, my back snuggled up to Jasper. We had spent our shared day off sleeping in and after a late breakfast, Jasper and I had started working on my room. We pulled all the furniture out of the room, and started to rip up the carpet on the floor.

It had been a long day of goofing around while we made progress on our renovation. Jasper had loved my idea of a half closet half book nook. However, instead of it being on opposite walls, we had change it to opposite corners. Jasper donated the spare furniture to Jake's renovation plan for his guest cabins.

"When do you want to get married?" Jasper asked from behind me.

"I don't see a need for a long engagement," I mused.

"I agree," Jasper echoed.

"How do you feel about something small, here on the ranch?" Jasper asked, his strong hands gently untangling my braids.

"At sunset?" I suggested as he started to massage my scalp.

"How do you feel about a surprise location on the ranch?" Jasper asked quietly.

"Like what?" I asked, confused.

"I have a spot in mind. How do you feel about the location being a surprise to you?" Jasper clarified.

"I'd have a say in the decorations?" I asked to confirm.

"Yes," Jasper agreed.

"Ok. But only for the ceremony, the reception should be at the main house," I agreed.

"I can't wait for you to be my wife," Jasper hummed, pulling me close.

"Hubby," I whispered looking up at him. Jasper smiled at me, holding me close against his warm chest.

"We are getting married," I hummed as it fully settled on my chest just how much my life would be entangled with his.

"I can't wait," Jasper chuckled deeply in my ear. *I had no one to invite —at least no one I wanted there.* My family was here. My family was *him.*

"Are we going too fast? There is so much we still need to figure out," I admitted, twisting in his arms to face the rough man holding me. He was like a mountain range, rough and raw, carved from the earth itself.

"We have time to figure it out together," Jasper reassured me. We fell into a comfortable silence, all the unanswered questions swimming in my brain.

"Do you still want to be a ranch hand?" Jasper asked, after some time passed.

"I do. I don't want our relationship to change work," I admitted, and maybe it was stupid. I didn't want my relationship with him to advance my work, I wanted to work to the bone and be recognized for that, and not who's dick I was bouncing on. Jasper nodded against my hair. Maybe he understood. He had spent many years working as a ranch hand, even though it was his family ranch.

"Do you want kids?" I asked slowly. I had finally found the courage to ask him. Jasper made several sounds as he started to answer and then stopped, unable to form words.

"If kids are in my future, I will be happily blessed, if they are not, our family as it is, is enough for me. Are kids something you want?" Jasper asked in return, choosing his words carefully.

"At some point kids would be nice," I admitted shyly. Jasper chuckled brushing a scratchy kiss to my cheek.

"Not any time soon though," I added, realizing he may have mistaken me. "I'm sure kids will come when we are ready for them," Jasper chuckled again.

"No telling your mother!" I warned him smiling. "Oh, fuck no! We would never have any peace over her asking for grand-babies," Jasper laughed, the rich deep sound filling my ears.

"I will not lie," Jasper whispered in my ear as his arms looped around me, his palms on my stomach.

"I like the idea of you carrying my child," Jasper mussed his thigh brushing over my lower abdomen.

"I mean, we could always practice," I giggled pressing my ass into his dick.

"I do like the sound of that," Jasper brushed his lips down my neck and over my shoulder.

My skin prickled with sweat as I pushed the wheel barrow down the barn. *Fuck, my back ached.*

"Sparrow!" Caleb came running around the corner, calling my name. How that man was still as thin as a twig while working here, I didn't know. I knew he ate a ton.

"Yes?" I set the wheelbarrow down, looking at him.

"Shit is going down," Caleb huffed, pointing over his shoulder. Caleb turned and bolted without an explanation. I ran after him through the barn, down the dirt drive and into his car.

Caleb drove recklessly towards the main house, and then round to the front and down the drive towards the road. Jasper's truck sat parked in the middle of the drive blocking it, and a black car had tried to turn in. My heart skipped at the sight of the car —no one in this county would drive a car like that. But it was exactly the type of car my uncle would drive.

At the thought that my uncle would drive such a car, I was back to the little girl I used to be. *Traumatized and never good enough.* I froze, dust pooling around my boots. It's not him, it can't be him. He doesn't know I am here. Smoke filled my mind, the echo of it filling my nose.

"How can I help you?" Jasper's booming voice asked aggressively.

Caleb pulled me towards Jasper's truck, and past it to where Jasper stood his arms crossed, and feet in a wide stance. He was pissed.

"How. Can. I. Help. You?" he ground out slowly. Jett and Mr Harlow were jogging down the driveway towards us. Still no answer came from the person in the car. As Jett and Mr Harlow joined Caleb and I, the driver's side door opened.

"Morning," a tall business-man said, smiling, adjusting his suit jacket. *My uncle.*

He walked closer his tailored, suit making him look younger. He looked polished —far from the truth.

"How can I help you?" Jasper ground out, the words nothing but a threat.

"I'm just here to talk with my niece," my uncle answered, flashing his salesman smile at Jasper. His teeth were unnaturally white and straight —it gave him a Mr. Potato Man look.

"And you are?" Mr Harlow asked with a little bit more tact than his son.

"Mr Montgomery," my uncle answered, not moving from his place by his car. I stood frozen, the leather of my boots creaking as my legs fought to run from the nightmare before me.

"As in the Montgomery's of Clarity Mountain Racing and Rehab?" Jett asked, frowning.

"The one and only," my uncle boasted proudly. Being one of the top racing, training, and rehab facilities for horses in Ontario, everyone in the horse world knew of them —and my uncle never let anyone forget it.

"A pleasure," Mr Harlow grunted, extending his hand —which was dirty given he had been working all day. My uncle looked at the rough palm of the man before him. With a hidden grimace my uncle shook Mr Harlow's hand with his smooth manicured one.

"You said you were visiting your niece?" Mr Harlow asked as he pulled his hand from my uncles.

"Yes, she has been working here for a while," my uncle said, the flash of anger in his eye unmistakable.

"I had no idea," Mr Harlow said, forcing a smile to his lips.

"We haven't talked in some time. You know young people think they know everything and run off half-cocked, their brains going with whatever impulsive thought they have," my uncle chuckled, the insult hanging in the air as he pulled a pack of disinfectant wipes out of his car. He took the time to clean the nonexistent dirt from his hands.

"Right, Sparrow?" my uncle asked, not looking up at me.

"Uncle," I finally managed to get out past the block in my throat. Every pair of eyes went from looking at my uncle to looking at me. I had run away from my Montgomery name ever since I was eighteen, and now it was staring back at me from my fathers eyes, in my uncles face.

"I have nothing to say to you," I argued, before starting to turn from him.

"That's no way to talk to me, girl. I haven't seen you in four years, and anyways I heard you got engaged. Don't forget who raised you," my uncle snapped, stopping me in my tracks.

"Why don't you come up to the main house? I will make some coffee and we can all sit down and have a chat," Mr Harlow offered, waving his hand towards the main house.

My eyes slowly slid over to Jasper who was looking at me, his eyes a dark storm. I panicked and bolted from him, following Mr Harlow and my uncle towards the house. My guilt trailed behind me like a tether to the man following behind me. By the time we made it to the main house, Jasper had caught up to me. He marched beside me not looking at me, but he paused at the front door and opened it for me.

"I need a minute alone," I whispered, avoiding his burning gaze.

"Five minutes, then I am coming to get you," he whispered in a deep grovel before he turned from me and walked into the house, where my uncle stood talking to Mr Harlow. I took a couple steps away from the house, sucking in deep breaths and trying desperately to get some fresh air. Every breath hurt. The fresh afternoon air was thick in my throat, ash coating my tongue.

I stood looking through the window, my eyes watching my uncle as Jasper stood there talking to him. His whole body was tense. I was physically standing in front of the main house at Swallow Road Ranch, but mentally I was back standing in front of my uncle's barn as it burned to the ground.

16 year old Sparrow

I stared down at the garbage bag I was holding. The new boots I had gotten for Christmas sat on the top. The memory of my uncle ripping them from my hands just two days ago rippled through my numb brain. The words he had muttered in his distant, cold voice — 'you will get them back when you stop acting like a brat'. Clearly, since he had thrown out the shoes, he never intended to return them. He had given them to me for Christmas. It was the last of the many gifts he had given me. All of them had been taken away over the last several months. I hadn't gotten any of them back —and know I knew why.

I fished the boots out of the trash and tucked them under my arm. I took the trash out and then headed over to the barn. I tucked my confiscated boots in a back corner of Cranberries stall. Tears burned bitter in my eyes as I nuzzled into Cranberries soft face. "I miss you dad," I whispered into Cranberries.

I trudged back, and slipped into the silent house. The newly renovated house had the fake country forced 'homey' feel. Cranberries was my home. The only piece of my father I had left.

I sat at the dining room table working through my homework. I had changed from my school uniform and into my barn-wear, already itching to go spend time with Cranberries. I scowled down at the textbook spread out before me. "Sparrow! Quick, help! The barn is on fire!" My uncle yelled as he ran through the house past me and towards the barn.

I bolted after him, panic gripping my chest, my heart thundering in my ears. I ate up the dust road down to the barn, and my eyes stung as the dirt kicked up around me. I rounded the corner, the dark billows of smoke greeting me before I even saw the barn.

My uncle stood with his back to me, his arms crossed, stance wide. I barreled past him and towards the open door of the barn.

"Sparrow!" my uncle yelled unconvincingly as I rushed past him. I tucked my shirt over my nose, throwing my arm over my face to shield me from the

heat. I ran past open stall door after door, all of them empty. As I ran deeper into the barn I passed panicked horse after horse, each of which bolted in the opposite direction to me.

Cranberries stall was at the far end, where the flames seemed to be spilling out of. The air was thick and hot around me. I blinked back tears as I stumbled to the ground choking. I crawled towards the stall I could barely make out the large black shape thrashing around in the flames billowing out of the stall. Cranberries.

I couldn't make it all the way over to the locked stall door to get it open. The only locked door in the barn. Flames were loud. The crackling of the flames, the bursting of the wood, the sizzling, and the sound of Cranberries screaming in pain.

Large hands landed on my shoulders as I tried to crawl closer to Cranberries. If only I could get to her. I could save her. The hands on my shoulders gripped me tighter and pulled at my arms.

Now

The echo of my screams as I was dragged kicking and fighting out of the barn by a firefighter bounced round my head at the memory. That firefighter had saved my life, and at the time I had hated it. I had been forced to stand by my uncle as we watched the barn burn to the ground.

We spent the next day rounding up the loose horses —not a single one hurt — except for Cranberries. *My stupid uncle* couldn't keep his mouth shut. Not twelve hours later, he scolded me, using Cranberries death as a reminder of my bad behaviour. *He had lit the fire.* No wonder all the stable doors for his horses were open.

"Sunflower?" Jasper asked softly.

"What?" I started, turning to him. *When had he got here?* I looked over to the house where I had last seen him.

"You ok?" he asked frowning with concern at me. I nodded, fighting to bring my mind to the present.

"You sure?" Jasper pressed, stepping closer to me.

"He is up to something," I mumbled looking towards my uncle laughing in the window. Jasper took my hand as we walked back towards the main house and the monster waiting inside.

"There you are," my uncle smiled at me.

"What do you want?" I asked, slipping into one of the dining room chairs. I wrapped my hands around the mug of coffee Mama H set in front of me, waiting to hear what my uncle had to say.

"I just wanted to come see how you were doing. Since you got engaged out of the blue," my uncle snarked.

"It's not out of the blue," I snapped back. My uncle shook his head at my tone.

"I only just heard about it," he responded.

"You aren't a part of my life any more," I quipped.

"I don't like your attitude," my uncle snapped, back his mask slipping.

"Then don't listen and leave," I answered glaring at him.

"Still the immature child," my uncle insulted. I ignored the jab, hiding the long standing pain in my chest. I could feel Jasper hovering over my shoulder. I glanced over my uncle's shoulder up to Mama and Papa H —my future family seeing my past family tear me down. *Why would they want this mess in their family?*

"Is there anything else you came for?" Papa H asked. He sounded a little too cool and collected as he spoke.

"I would have thought a family man like you would understand," my uncle muttered darkly.

"Understand what?" Mama H asked, she sat down and smiled warmly at my uncle who seemed to soften at her confusion.

"I raised her, but she is a wild child. I let her run off and waste her time doing whatever she wanted. But now it's time for her to grow up," my uncle said all of this to Mama H but he looked at me.

"Waste her time?" Mama H asked again, keeping her face blank and inviting.

"I taught her to be a horse trainer. It's time she returned to the family business," my uncle leveled the last words at me like a threat.

"I have a job," I quipped, back.

"As a ranch hand," my uncle scoffed.

"I will never train another horse," I snapped back at him.

“Oh don’t be a fucking child about this,” my uncle snarled at me.

“Why don’t you tell them why I won’t train another horse,” I snapped at him before standing from my chair and storming out of the room. Childish or not, I was done with this conversation.

“Sparrow!” my uncle roared at my back as I left.

JASPER

The woman I love was breaking before my eyes. My Sunflower was wilting. I glared down at the cause. *Her uncle.*

"So?" I asked, looking down at him. Her uncle frowned at me.

"What?" he asked, most of his anger melting from his face.

"Why doesn't she train horses anymore?" I asked, crossing my arms over my chest. I stood over the now empty chair. I itched to chase after her, but I needed these answers. How did she go from being a horse trainer at one of the foremost training facilities in the province to being so scared of horses that she can't go near them.

"She is throwing a temper tantrum," her uncle waved me off. Ma frowned at this. Sparrow was most definitely not throwing a temper tantrum.

"Nope, that isn't good enough," Ma scolded the man in front of her.

"Years ago my barn burned down, she lost her horse in the fire. If she can't get over the loss of a horse, she isn't meant for this business," Sparrow's uncle snapped at Ma. That crossed a line. Pa stepped closer, crossing his arms over his chest, standing next to Ma and glaring down at the man.

"So, she was traumatized by the unexpected death of the horse her father gave her, and yet you think it's a temper tantrum?" Ma asked, perplexed.

"That's not what I meant," her uncle defended.

"So what did you mean?" Ma asked threateningly.

"She is an adult now. She needs to get back to reality," he sputtered under the pressure of my Ma. I stepped forward, looking down at the greasy man.

"You are the delusional one," Ma prescribed, pointing at him.

"Get out," I snapped at him, pointing to the door.

"And don't come back," Pa added, in a deep voice he had never used with us kids. Not even Jett when he landed his ass in jail. Sparrow's uncle spluttered, unable to understand that he couldn't talk his way around this. That he could not use his money and power to change our minds.

"She is your mess now," he snapped before striding out of our house and down towards his car. Before he even made it ten paces towards his car, I was off to find Sparrow. She was no longer in the house, she wasn't at home, she hadn't gone back to work. I could not find her.

I rounded the outside of the barn at a jog, desperate to find her. I dug in my pocket to pull out my phone —which maybe should have been my first step rather than trying to run around the whole property looking for her.

I looked up as I lifted my phone to my ear to call her when I spotted her. Sitting on the top rung of the fence on the backside of the barn. She was looking out over the land with a blank look on her face.

"Sunflower," I coaxed as I swung my leg over the fence to lift myself up next to her. I sat down next to her, pulling her hand from the sun bleached wood and into mine.

"He set the barn on fire," Sparrow choked out.

"What?" I asked dumbfounded.

"He set the barn fire that killed Cranberries," Sparrow's voice cracked as she stumbled over her words. Tears ran down her cheeks, she didn't look at me as she slowly pieced together the pieces of the puzzle of her past.

"How did he get away with it?' I choked out as Sparrow finished telling me what that man had done to her.

"I could never prove it," Sparrow whispered as she pawed at the tears running down her face and neck.

"I'm so sorry," I cooed as I kissed the top of her head and pulled her close. We stayed there till the sun started to set, Sparrow quietly crying in my arms. It may have been the most painful thing I had ever done. Sitting there in silence listening to her pain and not being able to help.

"Would you like some chocolate ice cream?" I asked quietly.

"Yes," she sniffled. I jumped down from the fence, before pulling Sparrow down with me and into my arms.

"Let's go, Sunflower," I hummed as we walked towards our house.

Sparrow

Jade and Mama H took me dress shopping in the city. We made a weekend trip of it, folding in my hen party. I was getting married next week. In six days I would be a Harlow. The family I was destined to be with. The Harlow's had been family to my dad, and now they would be my family too.

We were turned away from the first dress store as they didn't do short turn around dresses. The second place was a large chain store and they allowed us to try on the dresses they had in stock in my size. I had so much fun dressing up in the big puffy ballgowns, and sparkling mermaid dresses. Nothing was what I had wanted. While I didn't have a dress style in mind, I did have a feeling I wanted to feel in my dress. And like a kid playing dress up was not the feeling, no matter how fun it was.

The next place we visited was a small local dress maker —who sold only her own designs. The inside of the store was gorgeous and the owner sat down with us and listened to our needs. She took some measurements, before disappearing into her back room. Several minutes later, she came out with a rolling rack of dresses. We started to look through them.

I stopped on a certain dress, it was a mermaid style skirt with short bell sleeves. The dress was made of a gray lace fabric and a seer nude slip. This was the dress —this was my dress.

Jade was pinning back my hair with a couple of black skeleton hand clips. She had me in curlers for hours, and now that they were out, she was pinning my hair behind my head in curly waves.

While not traditional bridal makeup, I wore blue eyeliner and a dark gray lip. It looked stunning with the dress and my hair.

We were set up in a small upright tent like one you'd use at a craft fair, but with four solid tarp walls. Jade had taken me up here blind folded an hour ago and we had sipped wine as we got ready. As my maid of honor, she wore a deep blue dress and told me all my silly wedding suggestions were the most amazing ideas on the planet.

“How we doing ladies?" Mama H asked, ducking into the tent.

“Oh my dear! You look stunning!” Mama H gasped. Mama H was walking me down the aisle instead of any of my family.

We had found some silk that matched the gray color of my dress, and Mama H had made me a veil out of it.

“You got shoes on dear?” Mama H asked, smiling at me.

“Yup!” I stuck out my foot, showing her my shoes. I was wearing the white pair of Doc Martins I had worn to my cousin’s wedding.

“Nope,” Mama H said shaking her head.

"You gotta wear these," Mama H insisted, holding up a new pair of black leather boots —cowboy boots.

They were gorgeous. I slipped them on, walking around holding up my skirt, as I lapped the tent several times.

"I love them," I pulled the older woman into my arms.

"They are from Jasper, honey," Mama H laughed, hugging me back.

"It's time," Jade squealed, handing me my bouquet of blue wood-aster, wild strawberry flowers, and wild geranium. Mama H folded down my veil, obstructing my vision.

With Mama H guiding me and Jade behind me holding my skirts we slowly made our way up a small hill, along a narrow dirt path, into a fenced field, and across an expanse of grass. The soft sound of music hit my ears. I almost couldn't place the opening bars. The soft smoky voice of Jasper singing filled the air. He had recorded a low soft cover of Hozier's Work Song, his voice full of emotion and gravel.

Mama H gently tugged on my veil, pulling the opaque layer up and leaving the lace layer over my face. Our close friends and family were gathered around the simple wooden frame that stood before the pond. Papa H stood right under the frame, with Jasper standing beside him. Jasper wore a dark gray suit, in a matching pair of black leather boots.

He looked fantastic, the deep orange light making him glow. I walked slowly down the makeshift aisle with Mama H on my arm. Jasper smiled at me, his eyes glassy as he watched me come closer. As I reached my soon-to-be husband the music came to a close and Jasper took my hand. I stepped up to stand beside him in front of Papa H who was officiating our wedding. Our small group stood around us in a semi-circle instead of sitting in seats behind us. Jade stood almost right behind me as my maid-of-honour, and Jasper had Jett standing right behind him as his best man.

I turned and gave Jade my flowers, and gently set my hands in Jasper large ones. Papa H had adapted a standard ceremony to fit us. Once he was most of the way through his prepared speech, he pulled out a black and dark blue braided rope. We had opted into adding a handfasting element to our ceremony.

"Sparrow. While I wish I had known you since the first day you started here, I would not trade those six months for how we met. I thought my life was great. I had an amazing family, work I loved and the best friend in the world. Then you walked in, and I saw the world anew. You are my Sunflower, with you in my life I have turned towards the sun. You are the bright light and the warmth of my life," Jasper spoke through his vows with a strength I could not muster. Tears slid down my face as Jasper went on about how much he loved me and promised to forever feed me chocolate ice cream.

"I never thought I would end up with a cowboy. Honestly, I generally avoided dating cowboys," I laughed some of my nerves away. "But I will forever thank myself for giving you a chance, anyway. It was the best decision ever; coming to Swallow Road was my second best. I have not only found the most amazing man to love me, but the family I was missing. Swallow Road was home for my father, and years later it is home for me. I can't wait to build our family here at Swallow Road," I fumbled through my vows, punctuated with small sniffles as I tried not to cry more. "I cannot wait to spend the rest of my days with you, Jasper," I finished, looking up at him as he stood there with tears rolling down his cheeks, a massive smile gracing his face.

Papa H continued on, inviting the ring exchange. Jasper turned to his brother who held out our rings to each of us. Jasper held out his hand as I slipped the simple silver ring onto his finger. Jasper slipped the matching silver ring on to my hand right next to the silver band Mama H had passed down to us. With our rings exchanged, the only thing left was the kiss. Jasper smirked at me.

"Please remember your parents are in attendance; you may kiss the bride," Papa H said, laughing as he raised his hands with a flourish. Jasper pulled me close and dipped me over his leg as he kissed me. A long and slow —and mostly chaste— kiss, my hands cupping the side of his jaw as his arms looped around me, keeping me safe. A loud cheer erupted from our small group as everyone threw the dried flower and wildflower seed confetti at us. Instead of a walk out of the church to an awaiting car that would take us to our reception, our group swarmed in on us giving the both of us the largest group hug.

Well, everyone but Jake and his date, Sky. Jake hadn't fully regained his strength from his car crash, and the only reason he was able to attend was because his date, Sky, was actually his physical therapist, there not for romance, but to ensure he didn't re-injure himself.

"Come here," Mama H called as she rushed back towards the tent. From a hidden corner she pulled out a large cardboard box. As she pulled out the box, it made strange slapping noises as what was in the box moved around. Jasper and I both looked into the box as Mama H opened it up slowly.

Inside were four adult ducks. Carefully, Jasper, Mama H, Jade and I all picked up a duck and walked with it towards the pond. We all carefully let the ducks go into the shallow edge of the pond. Each of the ducks swam deeper into the pond, investigating their new home. As a group we all made our way to the main house in the warm evening air. Jake and Sky had disappeared from the group at some point — I didn't remember them leaving.

Once we were at the main house, food, music and dancing filled the night. Our small group was joined by our extended friends for the reception, including some of my family members who hadn't been tainted by my uncle. Who was still working to ruin me within my family.

~

"Good morning Mrs Harlow," Jasper's sleepy voice woke me the next morning. It had been a late night and we had slept in well past noon. The bright mid-day light streamed into our room. I rolled over into the warm arms of my husband. *My husband.*

"Ready for our honeymoon?" Jasper asked as he pressed lazy kisses to my bare shoulder.

"Yes," I hummed, melting into his body. We were heading out on a road trip across Canada for our honeymoon, ending up spending a week in the Rockies before flying home again. Neither of us particularly wanted to spend our honeymoon flying around the globe, but a slow trip across Canada and a week locked in a remote cabin was exactly what we wanted.

"Let's go husband," I said, smiling as I sat up, excited to celebrate the rest of our lives together.

Epilogue

2 months later

Jasper

I watched Sparrow dance on the dance floor, just like that first night all that time ago. She was just as carefree and wild. If not more so, knowing that she didn't have to pay attention to her surroundings. I watched her, and if anyone were to try anything I would put an end to it before anything started. No one fucked with my wife. *Mrs Harlow.*

"I told you so," Noah chuckled beside me.

"What?" I asked, turning to him.

"I told you, you needed to get laid. You got laid, and now you are happy," Noah snickered into his beer.

"So my whole marriage is due to you," I bantered at him, turning to my wife who had her hands in her hair.

"You are welcome," Noah boasted proudly. I shook my head, laughing at my idiotic friend.

"You are buying the next round," I jabbed, as I threw back the rest of my whiskey. Noah protested until the bartender walked up to our section of the bar. She was new; I hadn't seen her here before.

"You need to get laid," I snickered into his ear before getting up and joining my wife on the dance floor, looping my arms around her and grinding slightly against her ass. I watched over her shoulder as Noah flirted with the bartender.

Sparrow

Jasper had his hands looped around my waist, his grinding on my ass paced to the music.

"I love you, Sunflower," he whispered in my ear. I pressed my body against him as we danced in the bar that started it all.

"I love you too. Truck?" I asked suggestively, grinding my hips against his cock.

"Soon," Jasper murmured in my ear. His head tipped up as he looked over to the bar where Noah sat chatting with the bartender.

"He really won't mind," I reassured, confident that Noah would more likely high five Jasper than be upset for us sneaking out for a truck hook up.

"He takes credit for our relationship," Jasper whispered, still watching his friend.

"Really?" I hummed, watching Noah as well.

"Truck," Jasper whispered, pulling me from the dance floor. I giggled as Jasper pulled me out the backdoor of the bar and round to his truck. I climbed in the back and laid down on the bench seat.

"Full circle," I whispered as I pulled off my panties handing them to him.

"Full circle," Jasper repeated, taking my panties from me.

Jasper and I stumbled back into the bar twenty minutes later looking ruffled and happy —freshly fucked in his truck. We slipped into the seats beside Noah, who was still chatting with the bartender as she bounced around the bar serving people. Noah had a glass of whiskey sitting in front of him —which he slid over to Jasper with a smirk.

"What can I get ya?" The bartender asked, sliding in front of me.

"The special. The Vexed lemonade," I said pointing to the small hand written chalk board sitting behind the bar. The bartender smiled as she started to build my drink.

"Enjoy," she said with a wink as she set the glass in front of me. I took a large sip of the blue lemonade. *Oh fuck, this was amazing.* I groaned, tipping my head back before starting to chug the rest of the drink, the bartender laughed as she watched me. As I set the still cold but now empty glass down, a huge grin on my face, my eyes dropped to her waist where her employee ID sat pinned to the waist of her jeans. *Vex.*

I started to open my mouth to comment on it, but Vex cut me off.

"Don't even think about giving it away. He's been working so hard to earn it," Vex chided good naturedly, pointing to Noah.

"What?" Jasper asked, confused.

"She won't tell me her name," Noah grumbled into his lap. Jasper tipped his head back, a loud full bodied laugh erupting from him. Noah blushed slightly under his friends amusement.

"Did you know that we started in this bar because they were debating if I was a buckle bunny," I offered to Vex, guessing she would find the same amusement in it as me.

"That's fucking gold," Vex snorted, looking between the two men. I leaned over the bar to whisper in Vex's ear.

"You gonna put him out of his misery?" I asked, smiling.

"Oh yeah," Vex confirmed before stepping back slightly.

"Once he earns it," she smirked at Noah.

"Anything for you, sweetheart," Noah said, winking at Vex.

"Ah that's a good boy," I cooed at him, sickly sweet. Jasper coughed into his drink as Noah blushed again.

"I like you,' Vex said, pointing to me as she danced down the bar to attend to another set of patrons. Jasper and I spent the next hour drinking and egging on Noah over his attempts to pick up Vex, who with her conspiratorial looks at me, was definitely going to end up in his bed at the end of the night. At some point, Vex switched my drinks to mocktails which morning me would thank her for.

"My shift is over," Vex announced, dropping the wet towel to the bar top. She leveled her eyes at Noah, who had perked up at her attention.

"What do you say, Goldie? Want to get out of here?" Vex winked at him.

Coming Soon!

Kicking Stones

Jake's story.
In recovery from a devastating accident Jake Harlow is set on opening up his guest house. Fighting his way back to the strong rancher he used to be.
Battling the reality of his physical health
Will he walk away with so much more or lose everything he was?

THANK YOU

To my husband, thank you for helping my dreams fly. Your undying support means the world to me - and I will never stop thanking you for standing beside me on this road.

To my readers thank you to everyone who gave my books a chance.

To my husband [continued], who spent most of my writing time leaning over and finger fucking my keyword —all in good fun— I have this to say to you: gnsgljashwoefjFKWWEF 49IF^@FHE4

Thank you to my amazing Editor Gee! I could not be more thankful to have you on my team! You are just as much a part of the Swallow Road family as me!

Thank you to my ARC readers for believing in Sparrow and Jasper's story!

Manufactured by Amazon.ca
Bolton, ON

55356067R00173